Stepping into the strange, dark gondola for the very last part of their journey, Rose blinked drowsily at the glimmering blackness of the water. She gazed up at the elaborate buildings on either side of the canal, the palaces of the great Venetian families. It was late evening, but many of the buildings had lights showing, or glowing shutters pulled across their windows, and here and there a painted face shone out in the flickering light, or a jewelled mosaic pattern sparkled. Venice was nothing like London. The water seemed to change everything, making it shimmery and dreamlike. It felt wonderfully unfamiliar. And magical. A whole city floating on magic…

HOLLY WEBB

ORCHARD BOOKS

ORCHARD BOOKS
338 Euston Road, London NW1 3BH
Orchard Books Australia
Level 17/207 Kent Street, Sydney, NSW 2000

First published in 2010 by Orchard Books

ISBN 978 1 40830 449 5

A CIP catalogue record for this book is available from the British Library.

1 3 5 7 9 10 8 6 4 2

Printed in the UK

Orchard Books is a division of Hachette Children's Books,
an Hachette UK company.

www.hachette.co.uk

For Jon

ONE

'Cup of tea, Rose?'

Rose stared blankly at Mrs Jones, and so did the rest of the servants in the kitchen. It didn't sound such a strange thing to say, but then the cook hadn't willingly spoken to Rose for over a month – not since Rose's magical secret had terrified half the household.

Sarah the kitchen maid was sitting at the big scrubbed wooden table. She looked from Mrs Jones to Rose and back again, her round blue eyes anxious. Then she slowly passed Mrs Jones a cup and saucer.

Rose swallowed, her throat suddenly feeling tight and narrow with tears. Sarah too? They were really going to stop pretending she didn't exist? She sniffed crossly. Why on earth was she wanting to cry *now*, when they were being nice to her again? When they'd made her invisible, she'd pretended so fiercely – to herself as well – that she didn't care.

Mrs Jones pushed the cup of tea across the table. She let go of it rather quickly, so that she and Rose wouldn't have their fingers on it at the same time, but it was a start.

Rose slid gratefully into a chair next to Bill, the apprentice footman, who was grinning at her encouragingly. Bill had never minded Rose's magic as much as the other servants had. Perhaps it was because he was an orphan too, and that joined them together. Bill came from the boys' orphanage that was across the wall from St Bridget's, where Rose had lived until she'd come to Mr Fountain's house.

He'd had longer to get used to the magic as well. He'd seen one of Rose's first accidental spells, when he'd been sent out to show her the way round the streets and the shops. Rose had been so overawed by the grand dresses and smart carriages, that she'd strayed into the path of a gentleman on horseback, who'd tried to hit her. Strangely, he and his white horse had ended up covered in sticky black treacle. Rose still didn't know how she had done it. But drenching a toff in treacle had been a good way to introduce Bill to her magic.

Bill shoved the sugar towards her and Rose spooned a few grains into her tea. Her hand was shaking, enough to make the spoon jangle against the china cup. Sarah had even given her one of the prettier cups, Rose noted, lifting it to sip. Only Miss Bridges the housekeeper had the flowered china, of course, but this cup had a delicate blue edge. Rose drank the tea cautiously, in case there was something horrible in it, although she didn't think there would be – Mrs Jones couldn't stand wasting food, and tea was terribly expensive.

Rose smiled cautiously at Mrs Jones, and whispered, 'Very good tea.'

Bill smacked his lips. 'Strong enough to stand a spoon up in.'

Mrs Jones nodded graciously, accepting the compliment as her due. 'I can't abide that dishwater stuff the master takes,' she agreed. She stirred her own cup thoughtfully, and then looked up at Rose. 'Did Their Gracious Majesties take tea?'

'I never saw the king and queen have it, but Princess Jane did, with her breakfast, and again in the afternoon. Princess Charlotte had milk, sometimes with a dash of tea in it.'

'Pretty little dear,' Mrs Jones murmured fondly, and Sarah gazed at Rose in fascination.

Rose smiled into her cup. Mrs Jones had always adored the princesses, though of course she'd never come closer to them than throwing flowers under their carriage wheels. Even though their master, Mr Fountain, was the Chief Magical Counsellor to the Treasury, and attended on the king almost every day, his servants never came near royalty. Mrs Jones glanced admiringly at the newspaper illustration she had propped up on the dresser, which showed Princess Jane inspecting a warship. The artist had made the princess a lot prettier than she really was, Rose thought. She ought to know, considering she had spent several days disguised under a glamour to look just like Jane.

The strange, unnatural winter had started it, a few weeks back. Snow and ice had descended on the city with an iron hardness. As the days grew darker and colder, frightened stories about ice spells and dangerous magic had swept through the streets. London's magicians had stalked about their business, followed by hissing whispers.

In the midst of it all, a group of Talish envoys had arrived to discuss the peace treaty. The war had been won eight years ago with a great sea battle, when the gallant captain of a British ship had told his sailors of

the birth of a new princess, and fired them with patriotic valour, and an extra ration of rum. But it had been a close-run thing, and there had been no triumphant invasion of Talis. The great empire on the other side of the slender channel of water had simply turned away from Britain, and started to annex little bits of Italy instead.

It had taken years of letters and gifts, setbacks and tiny victories to get the peace this far, and the embassy were to be wooed with a grand banquet to celebrate Princess had Jane's birthday. But then the princess had disappeared, and suddenly there could be no party after all, and panic gripped the palace. The envoys would hurry away back to Talis, deeply insulted, and the chance of peace would be lost again.

It was then that Rose had realised that kings were not like other people. All the while he was searching frantically for his daughter, the king had been grieving almost more for the loss of his treaty, and the peace. He needed a princess – or someone who looked like a princess. Mr Fountain had reluctantly allowed Rose to put on a glamour – an odd spell that gave her another face – and imitate Princess Jane, until she was found. Rose still didn't like to think what would have happened if the princess had never been rescued. She might still have been dressed in a princess's skin.

The birthday party had been a disaster, despite the glamour. The Talish envoy, Lord Venn, had attacked Rose, telling everyone she was an imposter – and of course he knew, because he and his master, the strange ice magician, Gossamer, had been the ones who'd stolen the real princess. She had been imprisoned in her own doll's house.

Rumours of Jane's disappearance had been flying around London, and everyone was blaming it on magic. There had been protests, and meetings, and even a debate in parliament. After Rose had rescued her, Jane had appeared on the palace balcony before the frightened and suspicious crowd. Over a thousand people were gathered in front of the palace, and no one was sure who to trust. The king had drawn his daughter forward, and given thanks for her safe return, but no one had cheered. *Was it really the little princess?* everyone whispered. *Or just another fraud? Maybe the king wasn't even the king!*

Jane herself had spoken then, dragging Rose to the front of the balcony with her. Somehow the sight of the child who'd risked her life for their darling princess had swayed the crowd, and they had dispersed without a scene. But there were still dangerous undercurrents running through the city. Most people accepted that it had been rogue magicians who kidnapped the princess, and their own magicians were trustworthy, or at least as trustworthy as they had ever been. But the rogues had got away.

The atmosphere was jumpy and frightened, and it made matters much worse that the kidnappers had been part of the Talish peace embassy – even though the rest of the embassy had sworn they were bewitched, and the emperor had known nothing of the plot. Lord Venn had secretly been plotting to destroy the peace mission all along, they claimed. They had all been taken in by him.

Rose had disliked Venn, a plump, rude little man, but she had been terrified of his master, the ice-eyed Gossamer. Since the plot had failed, Mr Fountain had discovered some of their plans, and they knew now that Gossamer had been the ringleader, and the magician with the strength to conjure that dreadful winter.

It was all very well to say that Gossamer and Venn weren't really working for Talis – and the emperor had said so, in several flattering letters to the king – but if they had succeeded, they would have left England weeping for her adored princess, and filled with hate for magicians and magic. Magic that would be needed to win any war against Talis. If the enchanted winter that had frozen the Thames had gone on to freeze the

Channel, which had been Gossamer's plan, the emperor's forces would have been over the ice in days, and London would have fallen.

Rose had rather hoped that Bill would be impressed she'd done her bit for the British Empire, but she hadn't expected that everyone else would forgive her for being tainted with that *magic nonsense*, too.

But now she realised she had underestimated the fascination of palace gossip. Sarah, who had been terrified of Rose before she left for the palace – she'd seemed to think that Rose might turn her into something small and leggy – gulped her tea, and asked, 'How many gowns does the princess have, Rose? Are they all embroidered with jewels? Does she wear kid gloves in her bath?' She held out her own hands, her short, rather stubby fingers reddened and scaly from spending hours every day plunged in hot water. As a scullery maid, she spent her time endlessly scrubbing pans.

Rose smiled at her. She could tell that Sarah was dreaming of the princess instead, stretched out in a cloud of steam in front of an enormous marble fireplace, admiring arms with kid gloves to the elbow, and heavy with emerald bracelets.

Sarah dropped the teaspoon she had been using to

stir her tea, and stared at Rose like a startled rabbit.

Rose gave her worried look back. Sarah hadn't just imagined the princess, she had actually *seen* her, probably on the shining surface of her cup of tea. Rose's magic had started that way, with accidental pictures. They tended to happen when she was telling stories, if she didn't concentrate very hard on stopping them. 'Oh… Where was it?' she asked huskily, hoping that Sarah wouldn't scream. Just when they had started to like her again! How could she have let herself get so carried away?

'Floating on the tea,' Sarah squeaked. And she hastily put her hand over her cup, as Bill peered over to look. 'She's not decent!' she snapped.

'Not in my kitchen, I'll thank you, Miss Rose,' Mrs Jones said firmly, snatching the cup and pouring the tea into the slop bowl. 'I've said it before, and you know quite well. That magic nonsense makes the food taste nasty, and it interferes with the range. Not to mention setting jellies. You keep it for upstairs, young lady, hear me?'

'I'm sorry, Mrs Jones, I really didn't do it on purpose,' Rose said quickly. 'Those pictures, they just slip out when I'm not thinking. I didn't mean to.'

Mrs Jones sniffed, and nodded regally. '*Does* she wear kid gloves in the bath?' she enquired curiously.

She gave Bill a warning look, one that suggested any silly remarks would see him removed by the ear.

Rose shook her head. 'No. But she does have attar of roses poured in her bathwater. Princess Louisa gave it to her last Christmas. And pink silk bath sheets, with gold embroidery. And Princess Charlotte has a toy sailing ship to play with in her bath, and *that* has pink silk sails.'

Sarah and Mrs Jones sighed appreciatively. 'And jewels?' Sarah begged. 'Dresses positively dripping with jewels?'

Rose shivered. She had only worn one jewelled dress: the silk confection that had been made to match a magnificent rose-pearl necklace, the king's present to his favourite daughter. By the end of Jane's birthday banquet, that dress had been shredded and covered in blood – Rose's blood.

Rose shook her head. 'Not jewels for every day. But the best fabrics. Lace, and velvet like cat fur. And no plain petticoats, lace on every layer.'

Sarah was nodding, as if this was quite what she expected.

Rose looked down at her tea cup, trying to hide her enormous smile, in case they should all think she was demented. The palace hadn't been what they thought. It was a strange, cold place. Even without dark magicians conjuring up the unnatural winter that had frozen the city in the coldest, deepest snow for fifty years.

There was no magic there, not like Mr Fountain's house. Even though Mrs Jones banned it from her kitchen – and her stern commands, strangely enough, did keep it out of the basement floor of the house – Rose could still feel it hovering close, waiting to enfold her. And now the hateful coldness from the other servants had melted away with the icy winter outside, she couldn't hold that silly smile back.

'Oh!'

Rose looked up anxiously. She hadn't let another spell slip, had she?

But it wasn't Sarah. The upper housemaid, Susan, was standing in the kitchen doorway, her expression one of disgust – as though she had found something horrible on her shoes.

'You came back. What a pity,' she snarled.

She was sounding brave, but Rose noticed she was lurking in the doorway, and making no move to come further in. Susan had always hated Rose, and the magic had made it a hundred times worse. It didn't help that Rose and Susan had fought shortly before Rose left for the palace. Susan had grabbed her, and – she had no idea how – Rose had withered her arm black. It had gone back to normal since, but she knew Susan would never forgive her, even if the rest of the servants were prepared to put up with Rose's oddness for the sake of snippets of royal gossip.

'I'll stay out of your way, if you'll stay out of mine,' Rose said coldly. It sounded like a threat, which was pretty much how she had meant it to sound.

Susan walked into the kitchen crabwise, edging round the walls and keeping the table between herself and Rose.

'She ain't going to smite you with fire,' Bill snorted, smirking at her, and Susan snarled back.

'Stop it!' Mrs Jones said sharply. 'No one's doing anything in here. Rose is sensible enough not to take advantage, I'm sure.'

'Freak,' Susan breathed at Rose, as Mrs Jones busied herself with the teapot again. 'Changeling…'

Rose shrugged, and smiled. She had a feeling that that would annoy Susan more than anything. The older girl knew how much taunts about her family hurt her, because Rose had let it show before. Rose had spent her time in the orphanage trying not to care about her parents. Trying not to wonder who exactly had left her in a fishbasket by the churchyard war memorial. And *why*. She had convinced herself it didn't matter, but now that she seemed to have

inherited something more than common sense and the plainest colour of brown hair, she wanted very much to know who it had come from. She no longer believed that she didn't care.

But those were secret thoughts, and Rose was good at secrets. She had been stupid before, letting Susan's words break into her. Well, from now on, she would be as still and sweet as stone, and Susan's sniping would flow over her like water. It was only another kind of glamour, after all.

So she beamed amiably at Susan, and had the satisfaction of seeing her shudder.

Rose had found it surprisingly easy to settle back into her life as half-servant, half-magician's apprentice, though she still found herself exhausted every night as she dragged herself up to her little attic room. The house seemed even busier than it had before she went away. Miss Bridges was determined that with Christmas fast approaching, the house would be spotless for the festivities. Mr Fountain liked the house to be decorated with holly and other greenery, and it did look wonderful. But it dropped berries, and bits of leaf, and small things scuttled out of it in the warmth of the house. It all meant more work.

Despite her extra lessons with Mr Fountain and

Freddie, Rose was still expected to do her fair share of scrubbing. Even her fingernails ached.

Her magic lessons at the moment were mostly concerned with scrying – that strange art of seeing things far away. Mr Fountain was employing his apprentices to help in the desperate search for Gossamer. He had escaped with all his powers intact, and they had no idea where he and Venn had fled. Or what they were planning.

Unfortunately, the lessons were not going very well.

'Have you found anything, Sir?' Freddie asked hopefully that afternoon. 'Any trace at all?'

Mr Fountain shook his head, and slumped into one of the chairs at the workroom table. He sat with his chin in one hand, twisting fretfully at his moustache.

'No magic – but then I wasn't expecting it, to be honest. Gossamer and Venn were almost impossible to pin down at the palace.' He laughed shortly. 'Hiding in plain sight, I suppose. Well, now they'll be hiding themselves even more carefully. I haven't had the slightest glimmer, though I've scryed for them all these weeks.' He sighed, a long angry huff. 'And not one hint from any of my sources. The amount of money I've spent bribing people. For nothing!'

He was surprisingly annoyed, Rose thought, considering that he could almost make money grow on trees. Mr Fountain was an alchemist, as well as a very powerful magician. Rose had never heard of alchemists before she left the orphanage, but now from what Freddie and Gus had told her, she realised how amazingly unusual Mr Fountain was. Alchemy had always been an obscure and slightly shameful brand of magic, simply because it didn't work. Until twenty years before, when Mr Fountain and his fellow student, one Joshua Merganser, had actually managed to turn lead into gold. At the time, Freddie said, they had been so poor that they had stolen the lead in question off a church roof, but Rose wasn't sure she believed that.

Mr Merganser had died in mysterious circumstances, and Freddie had told her some interesting stories about that too, which Rose really didn't believe – most of the time. Whatever had happened, Mr Fountain became the only successful alchemist in the world. But it seemed that now even gold wasn't enough.

'The trail is completely cold,' Mr Fountain moaned. 'They've vanished. Vanished!' He sank his head on his hand dramatically, and added, in a doom-laden voice, 'Which can only mean they're plotting something else. Who knows what the fiends are after now?'

The white cat, Gus, wove himself comfortingly around Mr Fountain's arms, and his master stroked him unseeingly, which was a mistake. Gus demanded the full attention of his admirers, and he hissed a warning.

'What? Oh! I'm sorry, Gus. Go on, you two. Show me what you've learned. Who knows, maybe it needs a fresh eye – one of you may catch a glimpse.' Mr Fountain didn't sound very hopeful.

Rose was just trying to open her Inner Eye to allow her True Sight to work, as instructed in *Prendergast's Perfect Primer for the Apprentice Magician*, when there was a knock at the workroom door.

Rose and Freddie jumped – it was almost unheard of for one of the staff to interrupt a lesson, as they were terrified of the workroom, and whatever devilish practices the family got up to.

'Come in!' Mr Fountain called, and the door opened, very slowly. Susan was standing there, white-faced. She thrust a heavily sealed envelope at Rose, who was nearest, bobbed the fastest curtsey Rose had ever seen, and ran.

'Odd girl,' Mr Fountain muttered, taking the envelope from Rose, and holding it out to Gus, who slit the wax seals with one unnaturally extended claw. 'This is King Albert's seal – what on earth does the man want? I've been at the palace all morning already. Really, this treasury job is becoming desperately dull.'

He started to read the letter, irritably tapping one

finger on the table, but as he scanned the heavy parchment, the tapping died away, and his face paled. Gus jumped into his lap to see.

'Oooh, visiting. And in time for tea,' he purred.

Mr Fountain shoved his chair back with a screech, Gus clinging onto his waistcoat and hissing.

'There'll be no fishpaste sandwiches today. Come on. Both of you, he wants us all there. Good God, how could this have happened? Why didn't I see it coming? Send for the carriage, Rose, and Freddie, for heaven's sake brush your hair.'

'What is it?' Freddie demanded.

'Those damned fools at the palace have *mislaid* – hah, that's how he puts it! – mislaid the magician's mask!'

From the stricken look in the master's eyes, and Gus's bottlebrush-fluffed tail, Rose could tell this was something dreadful, even though she still didn't understand. She shot out of the workroom, dashed down four flights of stairs and burst into the kitchen, gasping, 'He needs the carriage, for the palace, can you tell John Coachman, Bill?'

Miss Bridges stared at Rose over her pince-nez spectacles. 'Is he taking you with him?'

Rose nodded, looking down in dismay at her grubby apron and second-best dark wool dress, which she was growing out of.

'You couldn't do something to it yourself?' Miss Bridges asked, with just a hint of hope, and an apologetic glance at Mrs Jones, who was holding a copper jelly mould in front of her like a shield.

'I don't think so,' Rose said, after thinking frantically for a second. 'It would be a glamour, and I can't do those on my own yet.'

'Typical,' Miss Bridges snapped. 'No one thinks about appearances in this house. I've told the master. Well, we'll just have to do the best we can.' She bustled out of the room and came back with an armful of white cambric. 'I've had this put by. I had a feeling something like this would happen. Here, put it on, Rose. And just – well, just try to crouch a little, then your dress won't seem so shamefully short.'

Rose dragged off her apron, and Miss Bridges buttoned her into the new pinafore, which had lace trimming the arms, and embroidered flowers around the hem.

'From the look on the master's face, miss, the king won't care that I've got my old dress on. Something's wrong, I think. And I do have my good cloak. Thank you, Miss Bridges, for the pinafore, it's prettier than the princess's.'

Even Miss Bridges was not immune to princess gossip, and a small smile curved her lips for a moment.

'Run along, Rose,' she murmured. 'I don't suppose he's taking Miss Isabella too?' she asked hopefully.

'He didn't say so, miss,' Rose said apologetically, and Miss Bridges sighed. Bella, Mr Fountain's young daughter, was a terror, particularly when she thought she was being left out of something exciting, and she was expert at avoiding her governess.

'When that little minx starts throwing magic around the place, I shall be looking for a new situation,' Mrs Jones warned. 'She's bad enough on her own. I can't bear to think of it.'

Rose nodded, slipping eagerly towards the door. She wondered if she would see the princess again – strangely, she missed Jane, even though pretending to be her had been a rather odd way to get to know someone.

TWO

Even after living there, the palace was still a breathtaking sight. It reminded Rose of a cake – the sort of fine white wedding cake that the smart confectioners had in their windows, all crusted with swags of sugar icing.

An anxious-looking young man in an ornate uniform was pacing up and down the mews, clearly waiting for them, and Freddie moaned at the sight of him. 'Oh, no. Raph's done something awful again. Look at him, he's almost green.'

Raphael Cressy was Freddie's cousin, an equerry to the king. No one was quite sure how he'd ever been given the post, but Freddie believed it was because his regiment were prepared to lie through their teeth to make sure he never went near the front line.

Raph was startlingly beautiful, and so he was useful at the palace in a decorative sort of way – all Princess Jane's older sisters were in love with him. Quite unfairly, his good looks often got him out of trouble, but he was terribly dim most of the time.

Raph dashed to open the carriage door, almost colliding with the coachman, who retired to his box, muttering.

'Please hurry, sir,' he begged. 'His Majesty is beside himself with worry.'

'What did you do, you idiot?' Freddie hissed, jumping down, and handing Rose out.

'It wasn't me!' Raph protested. 'Really, I never went anywhere near the bally thing. His Majesty's waiting in the throne room, do come on.' He seized Rose's sleeve, and actually pulled her inside past the guards, hustling the party up an enormous staircase, the banisters held up by plump and winsome cherubs that had Mr Fountain wincing. He strongly disapproved of many of the king's renovations. 'The throne room,' he was muttering. 'It would be. All that scarlet carpet gives me such a headache, and the statues are absurd.'

Gus ran ahead of Raph, his tail waving high. He adored dramatic situations, and Rose suspected he was also hoping to finally have a chance to terrorise

Queen Adelaide's lap dog. Gus had been in disguise during most of their previous visit, and had been forced to control his natural instincts.

The king was pacing up and down the scarlet carpet that had so worried Mr Fountain. Rose agreed – the carpet was blood-coloured, and the walls were a shade darker. It was like being inside a bag of liver, which had been liberally dotted with gilded marble statues. It was also unfortunate that the king was wearing a crimson Guards' uniform which clashed, subtly and dreadfully. He looked haggard, his face greyish pale, and his eyes haunted.

'At last!'

'I'm so sorry, Sire, we came as soon as the message arrived. It's really gone?'

'Look!' The king wheeled round and pointed dramatically at a display of weapons on the wall. Even Rose could see that there was a rather unfortunate gap in the middle.

'Is this mask supposed to be there?' she hissed to Freddie.

Freddie shrugged. He looked put out, as he prided himself on knowing more about the palace than Rose did.

'Why are those *children* here?' Queen Adelaide was sweeping down the room towards them, the

train of her velvet dress trailing across the red carpet. Behind her trotted a grumpy-looking pageboy, carrying her fat little Pekingese dog, its eyes bulging at the sight of Gus.

'We need their help, my dear,' the king reminded her curtly.

Rose bent her knees slightly, hoping to hide the inches of leg that showed under her outgrown dress. But she could tell that the queen could see what she was doing. Queen Adelaide looked down her rather long nose at the two children. 'Do they have to look quite so *dishevelled*?' she asked in a stagey sort of whisper.

Mr Fountain bowed. He didn't like the queen, it was quite obvious – though he was far too much the courtier to admit any such thing. 'We obeyed His Majesty's summons in rather a hurry, ma'am.'

The queen's 'Hmmm' was masterly, and Rose and Freddie both attempted to hide behind Mr Fountain. This meant that Gus came out from around his master's legs, and leered at the Pekingese. The Peke stood up in the pageboy's arms and barked itself silly, while Gus merely stared demurely at it, standing decoratively next to Rose and opening his eyes very wide. He knew that made him look innocent, but Rose could tell from the twitching of his tail-tip that he was enjoying himself enormously.

The queen seized the Peke from the pageboy and cooed lovingly at it, but the little creature fought and scrabbled, yapping hysterically.

I think he is being terribly rude in Chinese, Gus told Rose admiringly. *I wish I understood.*

At last the queen handed the dog back to the pageboy, still wriggling frantically. 'I shall have to take Flower out of here,' the queen pronounced, frowning. 'He cannot stand to associate with such an underbred animal. I will speak to you later, my dear.' She processed out, with the pageboy following her, stuffing Flower inside his gilt-encrusted bumfreezer jacket, and glowering at Rose and Freddie, who were stifling giggles.

'Did she mean me?' Gus was staring after the queen, an expression of amazement and dawning horror in his eyes. 'Underbred? Me?'

The king had heard Gus talk before, but he still jumped slightly as the voice echoed from around his feet. 'I'm so sorry,' he said awkwardly – clearly finding it hard to address a cat, even one as grand as Gus. 'My wife is not fond of cats. I am quite sure you have a magnificent pedigree.' Tentatively he reached out to pat Gus's head, but something about the way Rose, Freddie and Mr Fountain all sucked in a breath made him withdraw his hand again.

'I am descended from an Egyptian god,' Gus snapped, his tail lashing to and fro.

'Sire, what is the magician's mask?' Rose asked, bobbing a curtsey in the direction of the king. Showing her ignorance didn't weigh against distracting Gus from clawing the reigning monarch.

'An heirloom…' King Albert gazed at the space on the wall, a dazed expression settling in his eyes. 'A mask, made of gold, and inlaid with enamelling and gems. Unbelievably precious, even as a jewel…'

'Except it isn't just a jewel,' Mr Fountain sighed. 'It's a magical tool, a Venetian mask. It's well known that the Venetians have strange powers, and they hold magical festivities, with *interesting* dancing. Rituals, you know. Foreign cults are mixed up with it all,' he added vaguely. 'Priests travel from the far Indies to be there, so I've been told.'

'Probably the ones that worshipped me,' Gus snarled.

'Mmm. I've often wondered about going to Venice. Masks, most fascinating things, and the Venetian masks are known to have incredible powers for the wearer… And as if that isn't enough, this particular mask belonged to Dr Dee, Queen Elizabeth's court magician. He was said to have learned many of his strange powers in Venice. Who knows what spells he

imbued it with, besides its own secrets? It's an invaluable magical artefact.'

The king, flushed spots burning along his high cheekbones, drew something out of his waistcoat.

Everyone stared at him politely. Eventually, Freddie ventured, 'That's a teaspoon, Sire.' He exchanged a worried sideways glance with Rose. Missing princesses were one thing – an insane king was quite another.

'I know that,' the king murmured patiently. 'Earlier this afternoon, one of the butlers discovered that the display above you now contained a teaspoon – this teaspoon – instead of Dr Dee's mask.'

Mr Fountain took the spoon, weighing it in his hand. 'It's been glamoured,' he said, tapping it against his teeth, and then biting it gently. 'The theft didn't happen yesterday.' He eyed the king thoughtfully, obviously wondering if he needed to explain.

'Well, of course it didn't!' the king exclaimed irritably. 'It was that cad Venn and his accomplice. Obviously! Who else has been dallying about the palace with unlimited magical powers? And look at the handle. Unbelievable conceit. The gall of it. They left their calling card.'

Rose peered over at the teaspoon, and Gus, curiosity winning over dignified fury, leaped into her arms to see too. Delicately etched into the silver handle of the spoon was an intricate snowflake.

Rose frowned. It seemed a lot of effort for Gossamer and Lord Venn to go to. All this for something that was just for dressing up?

'What will they do with the mask?' she asked, nibbling at one of her nails. 'Does it – does it *do* anything?'

'If they can unravel the secrets of its spells, they can do whatever they like,' Mr Fountain muttered, slumping onto one of the spindly gilt chairs, and wiping a silk handkerchief across his forehead. 'It's terribly powerful. But then, no one since Dee has really known how to use it. No one has dared to wear it, not knowing what would happen.' There was a strange longing in his voice, and his eyes were hidden by the handkerchief. 'I need to go home and look it all up – I have a history of Venice somewhere. There are rituals. Certain days when everyone wears masks. But this mask – the right person could wear it to wreak havoc, and remain a secret. Or, even worse, he could use it to create. To build.'

'To build an army,' the king said in a low voice. He didn't even bother with a chair, just sank down on the pedestal of one of the ugly gilded statues. 'An army of magicians, following the power of the masked man.'

'We wouldn't...' But Mr Fountain sounded doubtful, and he shivered, and smiled faintly, one hand

stroking across his cheek, as though he was smoothing on a mask.

Mr Fountain stayed silent for almost the whole of the coach journey home. Freddie and Rose exchanged curious glances, but somehow the silence infected them too, and they didn't dare to break it. Even Gus perched on Mr Fountain's shoulder and glared out of the window at the darkening streets.

Scrying lessons were suspended as soon as they arrived home from the palace, in favour of research. Which meant Freddie climbing the study bookshelves like a sort of trained monkey, dislodging enormous leatherbound volumes and clouds of thick, but somehow sparkling, dust. Most of Mr Fountain's huge collection of books were ancient, and many of them had no title on the spine, or only a few faded gilt letters. Mr Fountain was very little help. He sat in his armchair by the window, surrounded by rising walls of books, and occasionally peering out to remind them that they still hadn't found the *particular* book he wanted. As he couldn't remember the title – although he helpfully suggested that the author's name was 'something like flowers' – and had no idea what colour the binding was, Freddie's temper was becoming somewhat frayed.

'This one has Venice in the title, sir!' Freddie yanked the book off the shelf, and almost overbalanced on top of Rose in his eagerness. His arms windmilled frantically, and Rose's magic buzzed and shivered inside her, sending an army of dust motes swirling around Freddie, wrapping him in a blanket of grey fur. The vaguely hand-shaped dust-creature pushed him firmly back onto the shelf, and deposited the book in Rose's hands, before disappearing back into the faintest film of dust over all the furniture.

Mr Fountain blinked, and Freddie clung shaking to an enormous atlas that was so heavy he couldn't possibly pull it off the shelf. Rose sighed disapprovingly at the dust. Why on earth couldn't she have made the spell put it somewhere useful? Outside, far away, preferably. Now she would have to dust the room all over again, and she'd spent at least half an hour cleaning in here this morning.

'Mmm.' Mr Fountain beckoned her over, and took the book, wiping a finger over the binding and inspecting the dust.

'I'm sorry, sir.' Rose bobbed a curtsey. 'I'll clean it, sir, after our lesson.'

'I'm not complaining about the dust, Rose.' Mr Fountain shook his head wearily. 'I'm just beginning to think that you and Frederick could do with further lessons from someone whose magic works more... unusually than mine.'

'Was it wrong?' Rose asked worriedly.

'Of course it wasn't wrong. It worked! But I would never have thought of using dust. *Dust*, for goodness' sake!'

'What would you have done, sir?' Freddie asked weakly.

'Let you fall, I should think. You've been working on that secret floating spell of yours, the one you persist in thinking I don't know about, for quite long enough. You really ought to test it.' Ignoring the gobbling noises that Freddie had started to make, Mr Fountain added the book to his pile. 'That isn't the one I wanted either. But I think you had better come down until you have recovered. Each pick a book from here, and see if you can find anything useful.'

Gus slid sinuously around the study door, and padded across the Turkish rugs to perch on the arm of the chair, peering disdainfully at the piles of books.

'A fool's errand. We should be concentrating on Gossamer – find him, find the mask!'

'And what are we to do when we find him?' Mr Fountain stared at his cat, his eyebrows raised wearily. 'Walk up to him and ask politely if we can have it back? Don't you see? Rose only managed to defeat Venn at the palace by half-killing herself, and draining your power and Freddie's. And Venn was just Gossamer's deputy! He wasn't the real villain, just a weak man who broke and started to spill his master's secrets. Gossamer saw that his plan had failed, and chose to take himself and Venn away, before Venn told you anything else. We still don't know what he can do himself, and that's without the mask.' He stared out of the window into the square, but Rose could tell that he was staring through the snowflakes that were starting to fall again, this time a sign of the true winter. Fountain was seeing beyond the storm, seeing something – someone – far, far colder. A magician whose power matched his own, a magician who had not just one, but two dreadful weapons.

It was true that Gossamer had the mask, but worse, he had the ruthlessness to use it. To do anything – steal, kidnap or even kill – to get what he wanted. And they didn't know what that was.

Rose lay on the itchy rug in the study, leaning on her elbows, and staring at the book propped up in front of her. It was a most unladylike position, and Miss Bridges would not have approved at all, but it had been a very long evening, and she was tired. She eased her elbows off the rug a moment, hissing as the blood

flowed back into the woven pattern imprinted on her skin. Her nose itched with all the strange prickly dust floating in the air, and she had the infuriating feeling of being about to sneeze.

She stifled a yawn behind her hand, and tried to focus on the page again.

The fashions of the Venetian nobility are varied, and often quite distinct from those of the other European cities. Much use is made of luxurious fabrics, such as velvet, silk and fur. But the greatest difference in the appearance of the Venetian noble lady is of course her mask.

Rose's heart gave a sudden little thud as the word leaped out at her.

Many Venetians do not ever remove these strange accessories, or at least not in polite company, having an antiquated and superstitious belief that the masks are somehow part of their soul.

The most elaborate outfits are saved for the masked ball held on the first Sunday of the year at the Palace of the Duke, when the nobility gather to dance, and to participate in strange rituals...

Rose uttered a curse she had learned from Bill, and hit the page, and then coughed as a cloud of dust flew into her face. She didn't want to know about the fancy dress! What were these strange rituals?

'What is it?' Gus sprang down from the windowsill and brushed himself against her cheek. He lowered his head so that his whiskers skimmed the page, as if they could suck the words in themselves. 'Hmf. *Antiquated and superstitious* almost certainly means true, I should say. How can the masks be part of their soul?' he demanded, as Rose took the book to Mr Fountain.

The magician frowned over the book, flicking feverishly through the pages to find another mention. '*As described in Signor Fiori's odd little book*... Fiori, of course! Flowers! I knew I had it right!'

Freddie and Rose stared at him, looking confused, and Mr Fountain clicked his fingers irritably. 'Flowers in Italian – *fiori*. Remind me to engage a tutor in the modern languages as well. That's the book. And as Gus said, odd, but almost certainly true. Faded maroon leather, Freddie, about the size of my hand. Well, find it, boy! Go!'

It was easy for Mr Fountain to say it, but simply knowing what the book looked like didn't actually help. Except that now they also knew that it was tiny, and might have been pushed to the back of a shelf.

*

'Perhaps you've lent it to someone, sir?' Freddie asked wearily, as he shoved the last book back into its place. 'It isn't here.'

'I'd remember, I'm sure,' Mr Fountain muttered, massaging his temples with his fingers and scowling. 'Where is the dratted thing?'

'You'll have to go back to scrying.' Gus swiped a paw over one of his ears with a triumphant air. Then he gave a little sniggery purr. 'Perhaps you could scry for the book.'

'Oh, out, all of you!' Mr Fountain snapped, hurling a book at Gus – or at least close enough to make it look like he wanted it to hit the white cat. Gus jumped gracefully from the windowsill, and the book slid, spine sagging, down the glass.

As Rose looked back, the master was picking it up, stroking it tenderly, and the pages were sealing themselves back together. He laid it on the tallest pile, and sank back in the chair, staring out at the darkness again.

THREE

Even though Rose knew the mask was still missing, and they had no idea where Gossamer and Venn had got to, and that the master was fretting away in his study, she couldn't help singing to herself as she dusted the rooms, and blackleaded the drawing-room grate. The whole house seemed to have been infected with Christmas, as though the garlands of greenery all the way up the banisters had brought it with them. It was an entirely new feeling for Rose. It wafted through her every time she caught her reflection in the gleaming leaves, or sniffed the exotic spices that Mrs Jones had been mixing into the mincemeat. It was Christmas Eve, already!

Christmas at St Bridget's orphanage had depended

entirely on the generosity of benefactors, and they tended to give bales of cotton for new pinafores, instead of Christmas pudding and goose. The Christmas Rose remembered with intense pleasure had been the one where an eccentric old lady, who worshipped at the church the little orphans marched to in crocodile every Sunday, had given Miss Lockwood an enormous reel of maroon velvet ribbon. She had said it would be nice for the dear children to have hair ribbons for Christmas. There was enough for each of them to have a large bow, she had suggested, and it was clear that she expected to see the girls wearing it at the Christmas service.

It was lucky that there happened not to have been an outbreak of lice for quite a while, and most of the orphans had enough hair for a ribbon to be attached to. Miss Lockwood had gone about muttering about ridiculous luxuries, and how it would have been better to have had the money, but the orphans had walked to church preening. Rose had treasured that ribbon until it finally fell apart.

Christmases at the Fountain house, it was becoming very clear, were an entirely different kettle of fish, or perhaps oven of goose. The geese were in the chill marble-floored larder, hanging up most pathetically by their ugly yellow feet. The puddings had been made with great ceremony a few weeks before. Bella and Freddie had even been invited – although suspiciously – down to the kitchen to stir the mixture, and cast in sixpences, and a scattering of tiny porcelain dolls.

The grocer's shop that Rose was sent to so often had been full of Christmas goods for weeks. Boxes of dates were piled high on the counter, and there had been so many interesting additions to the jars of sweets that Bill took a good ten minutes longer than usual to finish his errands.

Rose didn't complain, for she took as long as he did, staring at the centrepiece of the sweet counter, which the grocer's daughter told them proudly had been sent for all the way from Bohemia. 'Which is a dreadful long way. Near to Russia, and the Americas, you know. It came by ship, all wrapped in tissue.'

Rose had seen gingerbread before, of course, and Bill had even bought her a gilded piece when they went to the Frost Fair. It was wrapped up with the handbill she'd had printed, in a little box under her bed. But she had never seen gingerbread like this – sheets of it, shaped and curlicued, and stuck with melted sugar into the shape of a little house, with a fence and a path of pink boiled sweets. Rose wanted to live in it. She could imagine tapping her way up that pink sugar path, to sleep in a gingery-scented, spun-sugar bed. She had chattered so much about the house to Mrs Jones that the cook had put on her best bonnet and been to the grocer's to inspect it, and had come home and sat staring at her favourite jelly moulds with an almost jaded expression.

Rose was giddy with excitement. She knew that Bella had even bought her a present, for the little girl had dragged her governess out shopping, and brought her back in a hansom cab, fainting, and whimpering about Bella terrorising toy shops. Since then, every time she had swept Bella's room, Bella had hovered around anxiously, and kept moving a small parcel from place to place in a manner that was meant to be secretive, and humming in an irritating carefree sort of way. Bella herself had written an immensely long list, and presented it to her father with the look of someone who did not intend to be disappointed.

Rose had made Bella a needlebook. She didn't think that Bella would ever use it – her sampler had been in her workbasket in the schoolroom with a rusting needle stuck into the letter 'F' ever since Rose had come to work in the house – but it was something, at least. She had embroidered handkerchiefs for Freddie and Bill, and, rather daringly, one for Mr Fountain as well, with his initials fetchingly intertwined. She had just put *Bill* on Bill's since, like her, he didn't have a last name, and only the 'B' seemed a little stingy. She should probably have put *William*, but it was ever such a lot longer, and she'd had the needlebooks to make for Miss Bella and Miss Bridges and Sarah. She'd bought Mrs Jones a quarter of chocolate satins from the grocer's and a doily to wrap them in, as the cook had said once how much she liked them. Rose had sat each night, gloating over her little store of presents, and remembering those awful weeks when the other servants had tried to pretend she didn't exist. It felt like a lifetime ago.

She had bought another doily too, to give to Susan. It felt churlish not to, and she had been well educated in Christian charity and forgiveness by the orphanage. Besides, they were only a ha'penny each.

Rose woke at her usual time on Christmas morning, but only because Gus clawed her. He had taken to sleeping on her bed, but Rose suspected it was out of affection for a warm body, not for her.

She lay shivering, clutching at the odd strands of the dream she had been having. A mask... *The* mask? She wasn't sure, only that it was white, and cold-looking, and horribly like the dead geese hanging in the cold room.

'Wake up!' Gus hissed in her ear. 'Time to go and light the fires!'

Rose groaned. 'Don't sound so happy. I know you're going to crawl back under my blankets as soon as my back's turned.'

'Of course I am!' Gus's orange and blue eyes were round with surprise. 'Why would I do anything else? Merry Christmas, Rose dear. Blow the candle out when you go, please. And tell Mrs Jones I would like a sardine with my cream for breakfast, since it's Christmas.' He gave a mocking yawn, winked at her, and burrowed back into her bed, leaving just a wisp of white tail showing.

Rose dressed hurriedly, huddling into the petticoats that she'd draped over her counterpane the previous night – there was no point in wasting extra covers.

'Don't forget the sardine!' a muffled voice mewled after her as she headed out of the room.

Rose clattered down the uncarpeted stairs, feeling distinctly unseasonal. The dream hadn't helped. She fetched her firelighting box from the kitchen – which was empty, though she could hear Mrs Jones and Sarah fussing in the larder, probably fetching the geese – and tramped back up the stairs to light Bella's fire. She was leaped upon as soon as she opened the door by a tiny devil in a pink lace-trimmed nightgown. 'Rose! I have a present for you!' Bella sang excitedly.

Rose gazed at her in bewilderment. She had known

that Bella was excited about Christmas, and giving presents, but she hadn't expected her to be like this.

'Open it, open it!' Bella thrust a prettily wrapped parcel into her hands, and jumped about while she untied the ribbons. Inside was a china doll, the size for a doll's house, dressed in a neat sprigged cotton dress, white apron, and a cap. It held a tiny sweeping brush, which was tied onto its wrist with a ribbon. It even had middling-brown hair, like Rose.

Rose had never owned a doll. She almost didn't know what to do with one, although Princess Jane had forced her to play with the enormous doll's house that took up most of one wall of the princesses' drawing room.

'Do you like it? Do you like it?' Bella couldn't stop giggling.

'Yes, miss.' Rose stroked the china features admiringly, smiling at the little rosebud mouth.

'It's going to be very useful!' Bella said, and she collapsed into giggles again. Rose shook her head. 'Hold her for me, Miss Bella, while I light the fire, won't you? She's too clean to be real, you know,' she added, smiling. 'I don't want coal dust on her.'

Rose kept the little doll tucked in her apron pocket, as she dashed about the kitchen that morning, and every so often she put her hand in to stroke the pretty cotton dress.

Mrs Jones was sleeping in her chair in the corner of the kitchen, recovering from sending up the most lavish meal that Rose had ever seen – most of which, she had been promised by Bill, would be coming back downstairs for the servants to eat – and Rose was admiring the little doll again, when there was a volley of shouting heard at the gate at the top of the rear steps. Two boys were standing there with a donkey cart, neatly painted with *The London Toy Emporium*.

'Delivery!' one of the boys bawled, when he saw Rose peering up at him.

'Run up and let them in the front door, Rose,' Mrs Jones said, straightening her cap and sighing. 'It'll be something else for Miss Bella, or that Freddie. Spoilt to bits, those children…'

But when Rose opened the front door, the boys staggered up the steps with an enormous parcel wrapped in sacking, and handed her an envelope. It was inscribed in delicate black ink: *Rose.*

'Oh, it's come, it's come!' Bella ran out of the dining room, in her best Talish lace dress, curls flying. 'Open it, Rose!'

So there, in the middle of the black-and-white tiled hallway, Rose undid the wrappings, and found her Christmas present from Princess Jane.

Her very own doll's house.

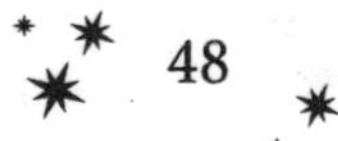

My dearest Rose,

Papa assures me that a suitable recompense will be found for your unusual service. And of course, it is the duty of any loyal subject to serve me in any way I should require. However, I wished to send you a token of my appreciation more personal than ten gold sovereigns and a framed picture of myself, which I imagine is what Papa's secretary is planning. I have conversed with Isabella upon this subject, and we felt that since you enjoyed playing with my doll's house so much, and since it played such an important role in the whole affair, it would be appropriate to send you one of your own.

With my most sincere wishes for the festive season,

Jane (Princess)

Rose sat back on her heels and stared. The doll's house was huge. Not by the standards of Princess Jane's, of course, but still. It was painted pale blue, but otherwise it looked rather like Mr Fountain's house – tall, with long windows that had little iron balconies, and steps up to the front door. *And so it should*, Rose thought, a bubble of laughter rising in her throat, as she had a doll version of herself to clean it.

'Isn't it lovely?' Bella asked, kneeling on the floor next to her. 'I chose it, you know. Jane made them send her a catalogue, but she sent me to the shop to make sure it was the right one. I chose my present at the same time, to go with it.'

'Whatever will you do with it, Rose?' Miss Bridges said disapprovingly.

Rose looked up at her worriedly. She hadn't thought of that. It couldn't possibly go in her bedroom – there wasn't room for Rose if she'd eaten too large a dinner, let alone a doll's house.

'Perhaps Miss Bella would let me keep it in the schoolroom?' she suggested, feeling guilty, although it wasn't her fault.

'No, no, it's yours!' Bella protested. 'Though I would love to play with it. It's ever so much bigger than mine…' she sighed.

'Put it in the workroom. On the window seat, perhaps.' Mr Fountain had given up waiting for his family to rejoin Christmas dinner, and was gazing at the house, shaking his head in amusement.

'Honestly.' Miss Bridges' lips were pursed. 'The most thoughtless gift. What do they think the child is, to give her such an expensive bauble?'

Rose couldn't explain. Miss Bridges was quite right, of course. The doll's house probably had cost the most enormous amount of money, and she certainly didn't have the time to play with it. But it was beautiful, and grand, and silly, and she adored it.

*

When Christmas dinner, and its encore in the kitchen, had finally been cleared away, Rose was allowed to run upstairs to admire her treasure. She found Freddie and Bella there too, eager to see inside the house. She was quite surprised that Bella had restrained herself from opening it, but she had clearly been admiring her present from her father: a most elegant, and enormous, doll. It had come dressed in a fur-trimmed evening cloak, complete with miniature opera glasses, and the rest of the outfit packed in a japanned travelling trunk.

'What on earth are you going to do with that thing?' Freddie asked, rather disgustedly, as Rose undid the hooks that let the front of the house swing open.

'She'll play with it, of course!' Bella told him sharply, indignant at criticism of the present she had helped to provide.

'Rose is too old to play, and when does she ever have the time?' Freddie argued.

But Rose wasn't listening. She was sitting in front of the house, stroking the Rose-doll, and admiring the tiny intricacies of the house. Plaster food, on delicate little plates. A painted fire, above small jewels of glinting coal. The little blonde girl in the nursery, with a proud expression so like Bella's.

'I think,' Gus said, appearing suddenly, and

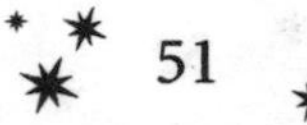

apparently out of the curtains, making Rose yelp, 'that she should use it. Usefully.' He settled on the roof of the house, leaning down to peer inside, and batting at the furnishings with one curious paw that set the nursery cradle rocking.

'What do you mean?' Rose asked, her voice suspicious, and her fingers clenched into her palms to stop herself shooing him away.

Gus's whiskers trailed a flare of silvery light over the doll's house furniture, sending sparkles skating over the tiny polished dining table. 'Practise with it. Spells. Scrying. It's like a little world – you can start small and build up.'

Rose nodded slowly, staring at her beautiful toy. It didn't fit into the workroom. Especially when there was an enormous white cat perched on it, although he did match the delicate balustrade along the roof rather nicely. It should be in a rich little girl's pretty bedroom, Rose admitted to herself, with a breath of a sigh. It shouldn't belong to someone like her.

All the same…

Bella came to stroke the silk drawing-room curtains. 'Don't you remember telling me about a doll you saw once, a clockwork doll that talked? And you hoped it was magic, because you'd never really seen any?'

Rose nodded. She'd admitted it to Bella while they

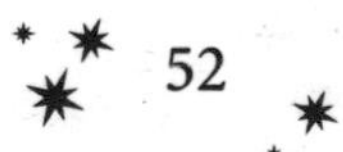

were talking about Bella's own magic, which was starting to show in her now. Rose had seen her grow claws, and she'd lent her power to Rose's glamour at the palace. But she was trying not to let on, in case her father found her a governess who would be more of a force to be reckoned with than the feeble Miss Anstruther. Bella liked being able to run circles round her governess, and she said she knew quite enough French verbs already.

'Well, we could do that! We could enchant this house, so that the dolls could talk!' Bella stared at it eagerly, her eyes glinting with a strange blue light.

When her magic starts to work properly, Rose thought with a shiver, *she really is going to be a little monster...* She shook herself. Bella was naughty, that was all. How could she be scared of someone who'd been so happy giving her a present? She stroked the skirt of the doll Bella had given her. Rose had put it standing in the kitchen, and it looked a little nervous. Rose shuddered. China dolls didn't look nervous. But she put the doll back in her apron pocket anyway.

Gus sat up on the roof of the house regarding them all smugly, his tail wrapped round his toes.

Rose stared at the perfect little house – the furniture rather disarranged by its journey. She picked up the tiny plaster gateau, one that even Mrs Jones would have been proud of, and polished it on her apron before replacing it gently on the kitchen table. More delicate things were packed in little boxes inside the rooms, and she opened one to lift out a delicate teapot. A whole dinner service was packed in straw underneath it. Rose laughed. 'Perhaps we should do the opposite of what Venn did to the princess. If we made this lifesize, I could go and live in it. It has everything…'

Freddie looked over her shoulder. He had been setting up his present from his parents on the workroom table – a clockwork train set. Now that the whole country was being covered with railways, an enterprising toy manufacturer had developed a child's version. Freddie had been caressing the red and gold tin engine all day. 'You couldn't live in it,' he told her matter-of-factly. 'No water closet.'

'Frederick!' Bella frowned at him. 'That is not a subject for polite conversation in front of ladies!'

Freddie only snorted, and went back to fitting his track together. Rose looked carefully in the bedrooms. He was quite right – she did discover a large china chamber pot under the canopied bed in the main bedroom, but there were no other conveniences. She patted the doll version of herself sympathetically. All those chamber pots to scrub.

*

'Bella's going to be awfully good at magic, don't you think?' Rose murmured, flicking away a speck of dust from the mantelpiece with a feather duster the size of her finger. Bella had gone to show off the whole of her new doll's wardrobe to her governess, Miss Anstruther.

'Awfully is quite right,' Freddie growled. 'Her mother was a magician too, you know. She made the most amazing charms, my father told me. She could get people to do anything. Bella's bound to be just like her. I'm considering giving up being an apprentice, I think I'd rather go back and live at home now.'

Rose nodded. Bella was commanding enough without magic – or much of it. 'Shall we try a spell?' she suggested, picking up a china bowl with a silken fern in it, which stood in the drawing room. 'Like Gus said? I'm not sure about bringing the dolls to life. It sounds a bit...wrong. But a plant. That can't do anything horrible, can it?'

Freddie stared at it morosely, and sighed. 'Probably not. Very well. You hold it, and think about flowers.' He cupped his hand around hers, and Rose tried hard to think about plants growing in the sunlight. Was it cruel to condemn a little plant to live shut away in a wooden house?

'Ow!' Rose opened her eyes to glare at Freddie, who'd pinched her.

'Well, that isn't going to help, is it? You're far too soft-hearted, Rose. It's only a plant!'

'It's alive! It might not like it, it's dark in there!'

'You can put it on the edge of the window, or on the doll's house roof when it's sunny. Take it out for walks, I don't care! Just let's do the stupid spell.'

Rose sighed, and let him hold her hands again. She remembered the wisteria that grew down the side of the house, now only a few greyish branches in the winter cold. She and Freddie had climbed down it once, to creep out of the house and visit her old home in the orphanage. The wisteria had caught her when she was falling. If she could give this little silken thing some of that green power, it wouldn't mind being a doll's house plant, she was sure.

She could feel Freddie joining the spell with her. He was thinking about climbing trees, and his mama's prized rose bushes, and the cucumber frame he'd broken once with a cricket ball. Rose smiled to herself, wondering how this plant would turn out, a climbing rose with cucumber-green flowers, perhaps. And cricket-ball fruit.

'It's working!' Freddie hissed, and Rose opened her eyes eagerly. He was right. The delicate silken fronds were shivering, and changing colour to a bright sap-green. Lacy tendrils were growing out from the plant's heart, and coiling themselves around, as though searching for something. One wrapped itself around the wrist of the little Rose doll, sticking out of the real Rose's apron pocket, and a faint greenish flush spread up her china hand.

'Be careful...' Freddie muttered, watching. 'Rose, I don't think you should let it do that!'

'How do I stop it?' Rose tried to pull the wiry green stem away, but it was tough, and sticky. An extra tendril shot out of it, and wound itself around her finger, growing thorns, and pricking her. 'Ow, Freddie, help!'

Freddie was pulling now, and she could feel him thinking about secateurs, whatever they were, and drought, and pruning. The little plant shivered, and the tendrils shrivelled away, back into the pot. A fingernail-sized blood-red blossom opened, letting out a sweet, innocent perfume.

'It's cracked her!' Rose mourned, stroking the thread-like craze over the doll's porcelain arm. 'Oh, and now I've stained her, look...' The blood was seeping from her prickled fingers, dark against the snow-white china. 'Freddie, can I have your handkerchief?'

But Freddie was looking down at the doll with a frightened expression. 'You don't need it. Look.'

The blood was gone, and so were the cracks. The china was smooth and perfect again, and the doll lay there innocently in Rose's hand, its painted cheeks now very slightly more flushed than they had been before.

FOUR

'It swallowed your blood!' Freddie hissed angrily. 'Of course it's dangerous!'

Rose shook her head. Somehow she was sure he was wrong. The doll did not feel frightening, or angry, or even different to the way it had before. Its face was still pleasantly plain, with that brownish hair – Bella must have searched carefully for that, as all the other dolls were blonde, or had shining coal-black hair painted on.

'It looks like you,' Freddie muttered, staring at the doll suspiciously.

Rose shrugged. 'She always did.'

'You have to get rid of it.'

'No!' Rose clutched the doll tightly. She had only had the little china creature a day, but already it felt

precious. 'Don't be stupid, Freddie. I don't want to, and anyway, what would I do? I can't just throw her away! If you're right, and she has got part of me inside her somehow, I can't let anyone else find her, can I? And if I break her, I'm breaking me. Besides, Bella would never speak to me again, and I don't want to make Bella cross.'

Freddie moaned, and slumped back against the window seat.

'There's no guarantee that its influence would be malign.' Gus stroked the tip of his tail gently over the china face.

'It's an enchanted doll!' Freddie wailed. 'It's horrible!'

'It might be useful.' Gus purred at the doll, and licked it delicately. 'Mmm. Warm. I do not think you can destroy it now, Rose.'

Rose cupped the doll close, protectively. 'I won't let you hurt her, Freddie.' Then she shivered, and shook her fingers, as though something had stung them, and stared down at the doll. 'She's moving!' she whispered.

'I told you! I told you it was horrible!' Freddie wriggled away with an expression of disgust on his face.

But Gus came closer, his whiskers a fraction of an inch from the doll, staring at it, fascinated. 'What is it doing?'

'She twitched, I'm sure she did.' Rose stroked one finger down the china face, and this time the doll moved enough for everyone to see. Gus sneezed in a sort of surprised amazement, and Freddie backed right into the corner.

The doll stood up, delicate china fingers gripping Rose's finger. It turned, and looked up at her. 'He's watching you,' it said, in a silvery little voice. 'He knows that they are watching him. The snow man. He sees you staring. He's hidden away in all that water. He'll pull you under with him. Take care.' Then it froze again, but this time with one hand held open, where it had been clutching Rose's finger.

Swallowing, Rose laid her down in one of the doll's house armchairs – which of course as a maid she shouldn't sit in, but Rose felt she deserved it. 'We need to go and see Mr Fountain.'

'You had better bring it with you— Ah. No need. He's coming.' Gus turned to look at the door, purring.

Mr Fountain flung the workroom door open, a bewildered expression on his face. 'Rose! Freddie! What is going on? I've just had the strangest feeling…' His eyes fell on the doll. 'So it is true…' He crouched down next to Rose. 'It spoke to you?'

Rose nodded, and Gus arched his back, purring and

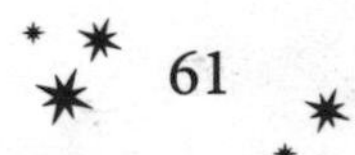

rubbing against his master. 'It warned her. She bled on it, did you know?'

'That's an old, old charm... A poppet...' Mr Fountain peered down at the doll. 'You'd better not ever let it out of your sight. I mean it, Rose. It could be used against you, terribly.'

'What did she mean? She said they knew we were watching, that they could see us.'

Mr Fountain sighed. 'They caught me scrying, Rose. I found them last night. After I sent you all away, I looked for him, in the snowflakes. His winter magic was his great strength, but sometimes, if you rely on something too much, it can be a weakness too.' He sighed. 'I wasn't going to tell you this today. It seemed cruel.'

'Tell me what?' Rose whispered.

Mr Fountain sat down, and took her hand, so that he was holding the doll, too. 'I didn't see where Gossamer is, just the feel of him. And his plans. Such a sense of excitement, and menace, and evil glee. He has the mask of course, His Majesty was right. But as yet, I don't think he knows how to use it. He seemed frustrated. Angry, almost. My guess is he's fighting with the spells to work out its secrets. I searched for him again early this morning, and it was easier to find him. I was so relieved, so desperate to see more, that I was careless.

He felt me watching him, and he was furious. His mind was almost burning with it. But it wasn't me he was angry with, Rose.'

'He wants the child?' Gus mewed sharply.

'Me?' Rose squeaked.

'Gossamer is still furious with you for thwarting him in his plan to steal Jane. It would have meant every magician in the country driven underground. Can you imagine? All of them, hurt, angry, frightened. Searching for an escape. Someone to rescue them. A leader.'

'You mean, he wanted us to follow him?' Freddie asked, creeping closer, though he still shivered at the sight of the doll.

'He was going to offer us what we deserved. After we'd been despised and imprisoned, perhaps we would have thought we really did deserve the right to take over. That's what he wanted. Magicians in power, with himself at their head.'

'He wanted to be king?' Rose asked slowly.

Mr Fountain shrugged. 'Why stop at ruling Britain? I see it now. If the ice had covered the sea and the invasion had been successful, he would have been the Talish emperor's closest adviser. His most trusted adviser. Which would probably have meant the emperor lasted less than a year. His heir is two years old, you know. Little Prince Leopold. Who would be the most likely candidate for Lord Protector, or whatever they call it in Talis? He would have been one of the most powerful men in the world. An Emperor Magician.'

'But we stopped him…' Freddie faltered.

Mr Fountain nodded. 'So he's gone elsewhere. He has the mask to play with now. Maybe he's given up on the idea of leading us all in some crazy crusade. He's going to find some other way of controlling people. Power, that's what he's after.'

'He's quite mad, isn't he?' Rose asked, in a small voice.

'Did you see any hint of where he is?' Gus asked, springing into Mr Fountain's lap.

Mr Fountain frowned, stroking Gus's white fur slowly. 'Water. A strong sense of water. But that could be anywhere! Probably he's on a ship, somewhere, although it didn't feel quite like that.'

'The doll said that too…' Freddie frowned. 'Didn't it, Rose?'

'She said he was hidden in the water, and not to let him pull me under,' Rose agreed in a whisper. 'Sir, if he felt you, he knows we're watching him!'

'He knew that anyway!' Gus's reply was scornful. 'Of course we are chasing him! All he knows is that we are strong enough to have found him, hiding away from us like some nasty black spider. A healthy fear, that's what we want him to have. Exactly...'

The white cat purred, soft and complacent, but Mr Fountain shook his head. 'No. Rose is right. I've warned him, don't you see? He'll put up more guards.' He thumped his hand on the table angrily, and the doll shook in Rose's hand. 'We need to find him. Now, before he has time to redouble his protection.'

Rose hardly heard him. The doll was still moving in her fingers, trembling, as though eager. 'Could I use her, somehow?' She lifted the tiny figure, supporting her sawdust-stuffed body under the arms, as though it had suddenly grown heavier. More solid. The little body twisted in her hand as she said it, and she felt the miniature fingers pinching her own. She sucked in a deep breath, and her blood seemed to surge and churn inside her, as if the droplet inside the doll was calling.

'Rose?' Freddie touched her shoulder, cautiously. 'She's cold,' he muttered. 'What's it doing to her?'

Rose slumped back into her chair, the doll held loosely in her hands, her eyes misty. The doll spoke for both them, its tiny voice clear and bell-like.

'It's taken him home. It wanted to go home. You really ought to read the book, I think.'

'Fiori's book? But we can't find it!' Mr Fountain

protested, and the doll shook its head disapprovingly. Even though it was moving, its china hair stayed all of a piece, the real Rose noted vaguely. This felt like a dream, but she was almost sure it was really happening.

'The chair! Think! When the chair kept wobbling! Rose, you should clean better, then you'd have known.' It settled back to being a doll again, this time smirking slightly, without her doll-like otherworldly calm. The tiny sweeping brush swung from a loop on its wrist.

'I do try,' Rose murmured, as she shook the strange fogged feeling away. 'But we've all been so busy, with Christmas...'

'Don't let a doll make you feel guilty,' Mr Fountain snapped. 'You'll need to watch it, Rose. Poppets can be tricky. It – it may not always have your best interests at heart.'

Everyone stared at the white china face, with its knowing expression.

'What's the matter with it?' Bella demanded worriedly, as she marched into the room. 'Why are you all looking at Rose's present like that? Rose, have you done something to it? It didn't look like that before.' Bella picked up the doll, frowning. 'It looks more *real*. Did you put a spell on it?'

'Not on purpose...' Rose admitted.

'You gave Rose a doll that swallowed her blood,' Freddie told Bella accusingly.

Bella stared at the doll, fascinated. 'Really?'

Rose shook her head. 'That isn't fair. The blood dripped on her, and I'd cracked her, Bella, I'm so sorry. It was one of the plants from the doll's house. Freddie and I tried to make it a real one, and...it went a little bit wrong...'

Mr Fountain glared at them both. 'I was about to get to that. Good Lord. What am I going to do with the pair of you? Dangerous magic exploding out of you, coupled with no common sense whatsoever. I never expected Freddie to have any, but you, Rose!'

'You mean a common servant child should have had more sense?' Gus enquired, his voice brightly interested.

'No! Well...yes. An orphanage upbringing should have made her very sensible, shouldn't it? Stop trying to tie me in knots, cat.'

'Blood will out.' Gus jumped off Mr Fountain's lap, and padded over the table to nose Rose's cheek gently.

Rose looked down at her finger, where there was still a tiny purplish mark.

'Not that, silly. Family blood. You may have been abandoned at an orphanage, but your family is claiming you now. You can't hide it.'

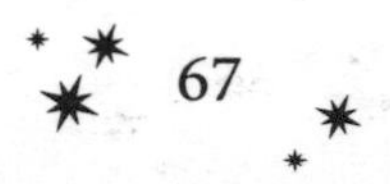

Rose ran one finger down his velvet nose, and sniffed. 'No, they aren't. Not really. The magic's just like leftovers. No one actually wants me.'

'Leftovers can be just what one needs in the middle of the night.' Gus settled into her lap, purring. 'Quite delicious. And most often, one can tell exactly what they were the previous day, too. I shouldn't be surprised, Rose, if we find you're quite the best smoked salmon.'

'Everything is always about fish for you!' Bella complained. 'Papa, I forgot. I was coming to tell you that most unfortunately, Miss Anstruther seems to have…' Bella looked thoughtfully at the ceiling, and then started again. 'She says she wants to hand in her notice.'

'Oh, not again… Bella, what did you do?'

'I only screamed. Not even very loudly. But she says her ears are ringing, and she can't stand me any longer.' Bella sounded quite proud of herself.

'She always says that,' Freddie pointed out. 'She'll be fine if you leave her to lie down for a while. Shouldn't we be trying to work out what that… creature…meant?'

Rose took the doll back protectively from Bella. She wasn't a creature. Although, as Rose examined the painted smile, she suspected that the doll had rather enjoyed being mysterious, and could probably have given them more of a straight answer. If Rose had wanted to. And had she really been neglecting her cleaning?

'Oh!' She jumped up. 'I know what she means!' She dashed out of the door, calling back behind her. 'Come and see!' She ran headlong down the stairs to the study on the floor below, and when the others caught up with her, she was kneeling in front of Mr Fountain's old leather armchair. 'Look!'

Underneath the carved wooden foot was something dingily red. 'You were sitting on it all the time! You must have used it to prop the chair up, when it was wobbling. I even saw it, when I was lying on the floor yesterday to read.'

Gus sniffed the book. 'I said you needed a new chair,' he told his master, his tail twitching irritably. Then he clawed the book out from under the chair leg, and flipped the pages over, sniffing at each one eagerly.

Freddie sat down next to Rose with a loose-jointed thump. 'You were sitting on it...' he wailed. 'All that time I spent climbing the shelves!'

Mr Fountain did at least have the grace to look rather embarrassed. He patted Freddie on the shoulder, and handed him a shining gold sovereign, which he'd apparently produced from behind

Freddie's ear. He gave Rose one too, although he simply took that one out of his waistcoat pocket, as though he thought she might not appreciate the conjuring trick. Bella looked at him hopefully, and then sighed.

'Ah…' Gus mewed. 'This page, look.'

Mr Fountain took the book and sat down in the armchair, which did wobble in a most irritating fashion. Rose could quite see why he had stuck a book under it. She and Freddie and Bella leaned over to look, and he read out loud:

'*Masks and magic are the marks of the city. Many Venetians wear masks all the time. Indeed, this humble historian has sometimes wondered if the citizens have faces underneath, but this is only a careless fantasy. Certainly though, the mask reflects the wearer, and the strange spells worked into the delicate things can change the painted face. Grief, anger and love can all appear on a mask, as well as they can on skin.*'

Rose felt Bella's hand creep into hers, and she squeezed it gratefully. She could hardly imagine anything more horrid than people whose faces were only painted on. Even though Mr Fiori seemed to think he was being silly, it sounded dreadfully real.

'*On the first Sunday of each new year, a masked ball is held at the Doge's Palace. Even those Venetians who*

do not usually wear masks will wear a mask for this event, for the sake of tradition. At some point during the evening, a secret ceremony takes place, and renews the strength of the masks for another year. Without the ceremony, the masks would wither away into dust, and with them, the souls of the people, and the power of the city of water. Or so the old story goes.'

'The city of water?' Rose demanded sharply. 'Does that mean Venice?'

Freddie gave her one of the looks he reserved for her stupidest questions. 'Of course. Really, Rose…'

'But that's what she said!' Rose pulled the doll out of her pocket, and tried to see some answering spark in the painted black eyes. 'She said he was hidden away in the water! And you saw him surrounded by water, sir, you said! The mask's made Gossamer take it home. He's gone to the city of water, hasn't he? He's in Venice.'

FIVE

'What better way to find out how it works than to take it home?' Mr Fountain ran his fingers through his hair, groaning angrily. 'I should have guessed. As soon as I scryed them with all that water, I should have known it. I shall have to go and send a message to the king. A sea crossing, in December…' He left the room, muttering to himself.

Rose frowned. *Surrounded by water.* Was Venice an island? She tried to remember the schoolroom map at the orphanage. They had learned the principal exports of all the major countries, but it hardly seemed useful now.

'If we're to go to Europe, it could be months of no lessons,' Freddie said blissfully, as soon as Mr Fountain had disappeared.

Rose gaped at him. 'You mean, he might take us too?'

'I should bally well hope so!' Freddie opened his dark eyes very wide. 'We're his apprentices, he has to. He'd be neglecting us otherwise. Think of all the lessons we'd miss.'

'But you just said—'

'Be quiet, Rose,' Freddie sighed.

Mr Fountain's message had an unexpected result. Later that evening, a very plain black carriage – so plain that it seemed particularly unusual, which was not the desired result – drew up outside the house, and an individual swathed in a heavy black cloak, with an opera hat drawn over his face, knocked loudly upon the door.

Rose, dashing up the stairs and through the green baize door, cursed visitors who came at suppertime, and opened the door with a pert expression on her face.

But it disappeared when the stranger tipped back his hat.

'Rose. I must see your master.'

Rose dropped a hasty curtsey, and backed away towards the stairs. 'Of course, Your Majesty.'

'Hush. I don't want it to be known that I'm here. I'm

trying to keep the disappearance of the mask quiet, and even the mice are spying on me at the palace.'

Rose smiled. She couldn't be so sure he wasn't right.

'If you wait in the master's study, Sire, I'll fetch him.'

'Nonsense. I can't waste time, Rose, I shall have been missed already. Take me to him.'

Rose nodded, and fled up the stairs, hoping to warn Mr Fountain, but the king was used to deer-hunting and other such energetic pursuits, and he was right behind her as she flung open the workroom door.

Mr Fountain was inspecting the tiny houseplant that she and Freddie had made, which now bore several disconcerting blood-coloured roses.

'How pretty,' the king commented.

'Your Majesty!' Mr Fountain looked truly shocked, for once. 'I had not meant you to come here, Sire! I was requesting an audience.'

'Walls have ears,' the king muttered, subsiding onto one of the rickety wooden chairs. 'Everyone in the palace thinks that I am having a most important conversation with someone else about the situation in Talis. It was the only excuse that would pass muster on Christmas night, when my older daughters and their cousins are performing scenes from Shakespeare. So, you've found them, Aloysius. I am impressed.'

Mr Fountain sighed. 'We were lucky, Sire. Gossamer

is angry, and that anger let me catch a hint of him. But it was Rose who gave us the clue we needed. Sire, we are almost certain that he has taken the mask back to Venice.'

'It would make sense. Please—' The king waved a hand at the other chairs. 'Please sit, all of you. Tell me what we must do next.'

'I shall have to go there, Sire. We think there is a certain day – a ceremony at the duke's palace. If Gossamer can be there, with the mask, he could unlock the secrets woven into it.' Mr Fountain closed his eyes for a second. 'If he does that, I'm not sure I will be strong enough to stop him.' He opened his eyes again to stare at the king. 'Sire, this ceremony is in eight days. The first Sunday of the new year. I must go *now*.'

The king nodded. 'A naval vessel, Aloysius. Whatever is necessary, you shall have it. You will have to travel by sea to Talis, and then over land, I should think.' He frowned. 'In fact it would be most useful to have your impressions of the mood of the country. Of course, they are all being most terribly polite *now*, but if Venn and this Gossamer fellow had succeeding in kidnapping Jane, and throwing London into a riot, the Talish would have been across the Channel in days. However much the emperor swears to me in flowery speeches that Venn was simply a lunatic and it was

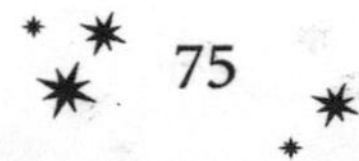

nothing to do with him, he is still mobilising troops all over everywhere. Of course he is planning an invasion. Then, you can take the new Trans-Alpine Railway as far as the Veneto… Venice, yes. Excellent…'

His Majesty stared into the fire, tapping his fingertips together. 'The Venetians have managed to preserve themselves as an independent state, even after the Talish occupied Genoa. An audience with the duke – if he should favour you with his confidence, Aloysius… How have they done it? How are they holding off the Talish? Is it magic? Or some strange trade bargain? It may be vital to understand.'

'So you want him to be a diplomat, as well as saving us all from this madman, Gossamer?' Gus spat. His whiskers were trembling, and Rose thought she had never seen him so angry. 'Do you not realise what you're asking him to do? He'll be lucky if he survives, and you want him to ask about trading agreements?'

'Sshhh, Gus. I apologise, Your Majesty. Cats are not known for their respect for royalty…'

'Quite.' The king stood up, and so of course everyone else stood too, apart from Gus, who stared insolently into the fire.

'Then I will let it be known that you are to journey to extend my compliments to the duke, dear Aloysius, as a fellow magician. I would rather not mention the mask at court, as things are so – unsettled. We hardly want to spread any more disquiet about power-crazed magicians, do we?'

Mr Fountain bowed, and escorted the king from the room himself, shooting a glare back over his shoulder at Gus, who turned his back on him, hunching his shoulders furiously.

'Is it really so dangerous?' Rose asked, in a small voice.

Gus sighed, and relaxed his spine into its usual graceful curves, settling his tail delicately around his paws again. 'We don't know what Gossamer can do. Of course it's dangerous.'

'Papa is the best magician in the world.' Bella rocked her doll in her arms, and glanced up at them all, scowling. 'He is.' She marched over to the window seat to play with the doll's house, as though she couldn't bear to hear any more of the argument.

Gus said nothing, and Rose felt a strange tightness around her heart. Did Gus think that Gossamer was stronger than Mr Fountain? Gossamer, who was holding Rose responsible for the failure of his plans?

The odd thing was, the tightness wasn't only fear. There was excitement too, and it was easier to think about the excitement. Rose seized Freddie and dragged him to sit on the hearthrug in front of the fire.

'Tell me about Venice,' she pleaded. 'Do you think we shall really go there? Why did the doll say they were surrounded by water?' She wasn't surprised when a light thump indicated that Gus was coming to join them. He was such a show-off, he couldn't resist imparting information.

'Venice is a city of water,' he told them grandly. 'No roads, only pathways and canals. Everyone and everything travels by boat. There's not a single horse in the city.'

Rose stared at him. 'Are you having me on?' she asked at last.

Gus rolled his eyes, and swished his tail into Freddie's leg with a meaty thump. 'You tell her.'

'He's right,' Freddie promised. 'It must be the strangest place. Hundreds of tiny little islands, all linked by bridges. Some of the houses have front doors that open straight onto the water – so you can only visit by boat!'

Rose eyed them sceptically. She wouldn't put it past them to make something like this up, to see how much they could get her to swallow, and then fall about laughing when she believed them. But although he was smiling, Freddie didn't have a hint of the irritating smirk he wore when he was teasing her.

'No carriages, or carts?' she asked doubtfully.

'How could there be, when there are no roads for them to run on?' Freddie pointed out.

'It sounds like something out of a fairy tale,' Rose muttered suspiciously.

Freddie nodded. 'I know. But it's true. And I think it is a fairy tale sort of place all round – the duke that Mr Fountain is supposed to be going to see, he's a magician, all the great families are. I should think it's only magic that holds the place together, the way it's all built on those marshy little islands.'

'And you really think he'll take us there?' Rose asked dreamily.

'Just like a girl,' Freddie said scornfully. 'She's daydreaming, Gus, look at her. We aren't going sightseeing, Rose! We're chasing Gossamer – the evil magician with the dangerous enchanted mask, remember?'

Rose shook away the visions of dusky waterways, and nodded. 'I know. But I've never been anywhere besides London, Freddie. I can't help but be excited.'

Mr Fountain stalked back into the room. 'Gus, are you trying to have me executed? He can still do it, you know. The act enabling traitors to be beheaded on Tower Hill is still very much in force.'

Gus yawned insolently. 'The man is an inconsiderate idiot, with no respect for his betters.'

'You can't say that about the king!' Rose told him, feeling quite shocked.

'He isn't my king,' Gus snarled.

'Stop it!' Mr Fountain sank into a chair. 'We don't have time to bicker. I must make a list of the travel arrangements. And it's highly likely that I need to find Bella a new governess.' He twisted his moustache fretfully, and frowned at Bella, who was leaning against his shoulder and gazing up at him, trying to look charmingly innocent. 'Why does everything happen at once? Perhaps I could offer Miss Anstruther a raise? I can't search for the right person to replace her now, I must set off as soon as possible – and yet I simply cannot leave you behind without someone to look after you.' He looked thoughtfully from Freddie to Rose. 'No, not even with you two.'

Freddie gasped. 'But sir! We're coming with you!'

'You most certainly are not!' Mr Fountain snapped. 'Do you think I'm mad?'

Rose's eyes filled suddenly with tears. She shouldn't have let Freddie convince her. But he had sounded so sure. Strange images of a watery city had been gathering in the back of her mind – without her realising, until they were abruptly snatched away.

'Sir, if you don't take us, I shall – I shall leave!' Freddie stood with his arms folded, glaring at his master.

'You can't,' Mr Fountain reminded him irritably. 'You're bound as my apprentice.'

'I don't care. I shall break the binding. You can't leave us behind. That would be desertion, and – and betrayal. Sir, it would be just plain mean!'

'I can't drag you across Europe on the trail of a pair of crazed murderers!' Mr Fountain yelled.

'You won't be dragging us, we'll chase you!'

'They haven't actually murdered anyone. Yet,' Gus pointed out helpfully, his sulks forgotten.

Mr Fountain shot him a disdainful look. 'Not that we know of.'

'Only that poor bird,' Rose put in. She still dreamed of it sometimes, the tiny racing heartbeat shaking her hands as she broke apart the shattered golden casing. And the fury that had filled her as that heartbeat died away.

Gus looked away, and Rose realised that he had probably killed rather a lot of birds. But that was different somehow. Cats were meant to hunt. Men were not meant to imprison living creatures inside jewels.

'We could help, sir,' Freddie pleaded. 'We'd be useful. It would be educational, as well! Think how much foreign travel broadens the mind. Rose needs a lot of broadening.'

'And I can solve the governess problem ever so easily, Papa,' Bella told him, her voice honey-sweet, but underlain with steel. 'You can take me, too.'

Bella's father pretended not to hear this. Instead he stalked out of the room, snarling at them all to follow him. Rose and Freddie exchanged a hopeful glance. Did this mean they were going?

Down in the study, Mr Fountain was spreading out a map on his desk, and muttering to himself. 'I'll need at least two days to pack everything I need. But I don't *know* what I need! This is impossible…'

'Which port will we sail from, sir?' Freddie asked, and only Rose could see that he had his fingers crossed behind his back.

Oh, please… she thought to herself, quickly crossing her own fingers inside her apron pocket. She was sure she felt the Rose-doll, who was pressed up against her fingers, give a little shiver of hope.

The master eyed them, and sighed, rather grudgingly. 'Dover. His Majesty seems to think there's a vessel due to sail on the twenty-seventh.'

'The day after tomorrow!' Rose cried. 'And – and we're all to go?'

Freddie glared at her – *Don't!* – but she couldn't bear not to know for real, not with all those floating churches and watery towers swimming around in her

head. Was she really going to see them? Would she walk alongside them, be part of the city of water?

Mr Fountain looked up from the map, frowning. 'It's your fight as much as mine,' he admitted. 'Especially yours, Rose. I don't want to leave you here alone either. I wouldn't put it past Gossamer to send someone after you.' He shook his head wearily as he traced a route across the map of Talis, delicately inked with pine forests and lakes, and a tiny, elegant tracery of railway track, spread across it like a necklace. 'No, we shall all go.'

'Me as well?' Bella asked, biting her soft underlip, and looking unsure of herself for once.

Her father glared at her sternly. 'This is not a pleasure cruise, Bella dearest. We are not just going sightseeing. One reasonably-sized trunk, that's all you can bring!'

Bella paled slightly, but she shook her curls. 'I don't care. Besides, Papa,' she leaned against him lovingly again, 'you can't leave me behind. You know that Miss Anstruther can't even begin to control me, and I'm sure that I would be worse if darling Freddie and Rose weren't here. I would be most terribly bored.' She smiled mischievously up at Rose.

'Sir, if you leave her behind, when we get back, Miss Anstruther won't be the only one who's given

notice,' Rose said hurriedly. She didn't want Bella terrorising everyone below stairs.

Gus brushed the map with his whiskers, and sniffed disparagingly at the railway line. 'I shall be travel-sick, I expect.'

Mr Fountain ran his hands through his beautifully groomed hair, leaving it standing on end. 'I'm setting off to chase a crazed magician with three children, a cat, and a governess,' he muttered.

SIX

As it turned out, the governess felt otherwise. Most unfortunately, when Miss Anstruther rose from her sick-bed the next day, she decided that she had, at last, had enough of Bella.

'She said that her affection for dearest Isabella had been finally overcome by the clever child being able to make her ears bleed,' Freddie reported to Rose. 'She thinks Bella needs more advanced instruction. And she said she didn't feel her constitution was able to stand accompanying Bella to Europe. Which is quite true. She'd be a fainting heap in the corner of the carriage before we got as far as Dover. I can't even imagine her making a sea crossing.'

'Is Mr Fountain still going to pay her?' Rose

asked. 'Even though she never gave notice?'

'I think he took pity on her. She did look dreadful, with a bloodstained cloth all wrapped round her head. He paid her wages for the rest of the year, too.'

Rose shuddered. 'If anyone deserved her money, she did.'

Freddie sighed. 'You do realise, no one will be paying *us* when we get landed with looking after Bella? In fact, we'll be the ones getting into trouble when she does something terrible. At least if Miss Anstruther had come, we could have said it was her fault…'

Rose nodded grimly. 'I'm already supposed to help her pack. She wants to take every single dress she owns, and she just won't believe me when I tell her they can't fit in that trunk. As soon as I have everything packed, all ironed, and wrapped in silver paper, she flings it all out again because I haven't put in her absolute favourite dress. Which changes every five minutes.'

Freddie snorted with laughter. 'Perhaps you should just pack her in there. It'd keep her quiet.'

Rose nodded, but she was frowning. 'How strong do you think she really will be, when all her magic comes in?' She stared down at her hands. 'I know Bella's a spoilt little horror, but I like her. She's sweet to me sometimes – she was so excited about giving me the doll.'

'You're talking about me again.' The honey-sweet little voice whispered in Rose's right ear, and she actually screamed.

'How did you get there!' Freddie demanded, sounding shaken.

'Simple,' Bella snapped. 'I walked in through the open door while you two were too busy gossiping about me to listen properly. We are about to set out on a secret diplomatic mission, you know. You need to be a great deal more cautious.'

'You are a deceitful little brat!' Freddie snarled.

'Do you realise, Rose,' Bella ignored him completely, and went on murmuring in Rose's ear, 'that when we set off, you won't be a maid any more? None of the servants are coming with us. You'll be a magician's apprentice, and nothing else.' She paused. 'You really ought to bring some better clothes.'

Rose frowned at the insult, but then what Bella had actually said sunk in. She had already gone from being an orphanage brat to a respectable servant, which was all she had ever hoped for. Surely no one would ever think she was anything more?

'Miss Bridges says I've to take this up to your room.'

Rose looked up from the china lamb she was dusting. Miss Bridges had looked so horrified when

Rose explained that she was about to disappear again, that Rose felt she couldn't really excuse herself from any more housework.

Bill was standing in the doorway of Bella's room, his arms full of some sort of shapeless fabric. Rose stared at it, her expression puzzled.

'It's a carpet bag,' he told her, scowling. 'For you to pack your things in.' He was silent for a moment. 'You're really going, then?'

Rose nodded. 'I have to.' It was almost true. It would not be kind to show Bill how desperately excited she felt.

'Why's the master need you, for some jaunt abroad?'

Rose held back – with difficulty – from telling Bill to mind his own business. He had no right to act as though he owned her. *You did let him take you to the Frost Fair*, a nicer inner Rose pointed out. *He bought you gingerbread.* The thought of the gingerbread, still wrapped in tissue in a box under her bed, sweetened her tongue.

'It's because of being an apprentice. We have to go, to learn things. We have to go where he goes.'

'I don't like you going off with the master, and that Freddie. And Miss Bella! You'll be shipwrecked, with her around. She's a monster!'

Rose grinned. He was quite right, but the monster

had given her three lace collars, and told her father that Rose needed more clothes. It had proved too late to order any, but Mr Fountain had promised to buy her a dress while they were in Venice. Bella had been grudgingly satisfied, and Rose couldn't stop thinking about it. 'She's better when her father's there,' she promised Bill soothingly.

'Huh.' He walked out, leaving Rose still holding the china lamb from Bella's mantelpiece, and gazing after him stricken. She put it back on the marble mantel, setting it down too hard. Bill was never like that! He'd been a little strange, when he first saw her do magic, but he'd got used to it. He was her friend, always. Rose looked at the lamb, her eyes watering, and saw in dismay that its delicate china tail had fallen off. It was gazing up at her mournfully, and the little shepherd girl who stood at the other end of the mantelpiece was glaring at her. Sometimes the magic all through the house made housework more difficult, rather than less.

'I'm sorry,' Rose muttered, trying to push the fragile china back together with trembling fingers, muttering some hopeful, sticking sort of words. It wasn't working. Bella would be furious. The lamb was now giving her a reproachful look, and the shepherdess had most definitely moved along the mantelpiece to see better. 'You do it then!' Rose hissed crossly, and the china skirts flounced. Rose scowled down at the lamb, and muttered again, but this time in a rather threatening tone. 'Mint sauce! Redcurrant jelly, and roast potatoes. Be quick about it!'

There was a whisk of porcelain fleece, and the broken piece was suddenly attached again. Rose set the figure back on the mantel, carefully this time, and made a face at the shepherdess, who gazed snootily back at her. Had her arms been folded like that before? Rose couldn't remember, and she hoped Bella wouldn't either.

Rose's humble little carpet bag was buried in a mountain of other baggage that was piled over the black-and-white tiled floor. She could just see a fraction of it sticking out, and she was twisting her gloved fingers behind her back, so as to stop herself snatching it back up. She wanted to clutch it close, like a little bit of home. She made do with stroking the little china doll in her cloak pocket instead. She had noticed that one side of the doll's face was shinier than the other now, from all the times she ran her thumb over its cheek.

They were going, really going! She had run to the receiving office herself with Mr Fountain's letter to Lord Lynton, the British Ambassador to the duke's court, explaining that they would arrive at the mercy of the tides. Now the strange words of the address kept dancing through her head, wonderfully foreign. Freddie had written them out onto dozens of labels for the bags, muttering crossly about the fiddly spelling. Rose had one tied onto the handles of her little bag, too.

Mr Fountain was proving himself a fussy and demanding traveller, and kept adding more and more luggage. An extra coach had been hired to carry it all, and its coachman and two of the stable boys were loading it, with Mr Fountain dancing around them, beseeching them to be careful.

'Be good, Rose,' Miss Bridges told her sternly. 'And please, if you can, try to keep control of Miss Isabella.' She glanced at Bella, who was standing out on the front steps, looking particularly darling and carrying her Christmas doll. 'Or at least, do not let her...' She paused again. 'I don't know quite what to say,' she sighed.

'I will do my best, Miss,' Rose promised.

'Come back safely,' Miss Bridges said, her voice sterner than ever, before she shocked Rose by folding her in a brief and bony hug. 'You too, Master Frederick,' she added, in a voice that was now positively doom-laden.

'Yes, Miss Bridges.' Freddie sounded surprised. He

had been quite certain that the housekeeper couldn't stand him, as he was constantly breaking things.

Miss Bridges rolled her eyes, and passed Rose a small hamper. 'Mrs Jones said you had better take care of this, Rose. And do not let that cat in it!'

'Potted shrimps!' Gus mewed in Rose's ear, from where he was perched, peering down from the top of the grandfather clock. 'Delicious. You really had better let me look after it, Rose. Perhaps I should sit on it.'

'Come along, children, don't dawdle!' Mr Fountain scolded, most unfairly. 'Miss Bridges, I know I can rely on you to take care of everything in my absence.' He flapped his travelling cloak at Rose and Freddie, shooing them towards the family carriage.

Susan minced after them with a pile of fur rugs, and Rose snuggled her feet onto the hot brick that had been wrapped in more fur on the carriage floor. After Freddie had got out again to fetch the travelling chessboard that he had left on the hall table, and Bella had found her purse in the pocket of her cloak, despite it most definitely having not been there before, Mr Fountain at last gave the order to drive on.

Rose, sitting with her back to the horses, could see just a glimpse of the Fountain house, and the servants gathered to wave them off. Even Sarah and Mrs Jones were at the top of the area steps, waving their handkerchiefs. She waved back shyly. As far as the servants knew, they were off gallivanting with Mr Fountain on a visit to some strange foreign place, where there was a lot of magic, and the master was gathering information for the king. Everyone in the kitchen had agreed it was just like him to go rushing off at a moment's notice, setting everyone in an uproar until he got his way.

No one knew that they were really chasing after a four-hundred-year-old mask, and the madmen who'd stolen it. The madmen who wanted to use it for some strange, cruel purpose. The madmen who'd rather like it to help them do away with their little Rose.

Rose pushed thoughts of the mask away, and tried to remember the eager excitement she had woken with that morning. She waved again to Miss Bridges, noting her troubled expression. She wasn't sure the housekeeper believed the vague story Mr Fountain had told. Susan was standing behind the housekeeper, staring coldly after Rose. And Bill was nowhere to be seen. Rose sighed miserably. He hadn't spoken to her since their fight yesterday, and this morning she hadn't had even a glimpse of him. She wished he would have come to say goodbye at least. Perhaps if she had told him the truth? But then he would have been even angrier about her going.

Gus gave a morose little hiss. 'Here we go. Cats shouldn't go journeying,' he muttered. The wheels ground slowly over the frosted road, and the carriage gathered speed. The grey horses made a fine show as they drove out of the square and set off through London, heading for the Dover road.

SEVEN

Freddie spent the first part of the journey trying to teach Rose chess. She didn't really want to learn, she would have preferred just to look out of the window. Already they had reached a part of London she had never seen before. Unfortunately, Freddie had been on plenty of coach journeys, and he wanted to be entertained.

After a few minutes Rose was sure that Freddie must be cheating, perhaps making up the rules as he went along. 'But why does the horse one move like that? Horses don't go sideways, do they? It doesn't make sense!'

'It's called a knight, Rose, and just because you're losing…' Freddie said smugly.

'Play with Gus, instead,' Rose snapped. Which was much better, as now she could hear Freddie moaning that he was sure that wasn't allowed, and that moving the pieces with one's whiskers was most improper.

Rose pressed her cheek against the chill glass, feeling the swing and bounce of the well-sprung carriage, and hungrily watched the road flowing away behind them. She wondered when they would see the sea.

The journey took a whole long, muddy day. Rose had never seen so much space before, so much empty ground, dark and frosted, and edged with stands of lonely-looking trees. She had thought she would love to see the countryside, but she found herself missing buildings, and wondering where all the people were.

Mr Fountain was anxious to reach Dover that day, so he allowed only the briefest stops to change the horses, with no lingering at the inns. Mrs Jones's hamper was disposed of at midday, and the smell of fishpaste lingered unpleasantly afterwards, so that Rose was glad to be allowed out for a few minutes to gulp at a cup of bitter coffee at the next change. She and Bella and Gus huddled by the coffee-room fire. The hot bricks on the carriage floor had long since lost their warmth, and the day was only getting colder. The afternoon was drawing in already, with pinkish streaks of cloud flooding the sky.

Bella fell asleep on Rose's shoulder on that last stage, and Rose was grateful for the warmth of the smaller girl. She lay back against the velvet seat, wondering how Bella could possibly sleep, and how the beautifully sprung carriage that had left London had turned into a wood-wheeled cart.

She woke to find Freddie shaking her, and the carriage stopped at last.

'Are we here?' She nudged Bella gently, shivering as she pushed the fur rug away.

'Yes, yes, come on!' Freddie told her excitedly. 'Come and see!'

Bella was still half-asleep, and leaning on Rose, so Rose climbed out of the carriage sideways, concentrating on not letting her fall. It wasn't until they were both standing on the stone dock that Rose took any notice of where they were. She stared up at the black *thing* towering above her, and swallowed. It looked so fast, so made for cutting through the water that it seemed to be charging down upon her, even though she could see the ropes tying it to the strange iron mushrooms sprouting from the dock. The ship resembled a shark, or one of those strange black diving birds that Rose had seen in Freddie's *Boy's Guide to Natural History, with twenty-four coloured plates.*

And they were going to sail on it. It was going to go

flying through the water with them on board. Rose tore her eyes away from the black-painted timbers and saw that they were surrounded by a forest of masts, all starkly black against the fiery sky.

Sailors were hurrying down from the vessel, and disappearing with the baggage, and an officer came stalking down the gangplank to escort them aboard.

Freddie was bubbling over with excitement at their luck. The naval vessel that the king had promised was in fact the very same *Princess Jane* that had had such a dramatic effect on the Talish war, he explained to Rose. She had been renamed after the baby princess, and regarded as a lucky ship ever since. Her original commander, the gallant Captain Fremantle, had most unfortunately been lost overboard while on a cruise to the Indies. The crew swore blind that he had been snatched from the forecastle by an enormous squid, but it had been felt by the Admiralty that this was untrue. Captain Fremantle had been very fond of rum, and it seemed more likely that he had simply lost his footing in a rough sea and slipped overboard. It was assumed that his crew, who had the greatest affection for him, despite his liking of long speeches, had manufactured the squid story to glorify his memory.

The *Princess Jane* was now commanded by Captain Peake, and Rose thought his memory seemed unlikely

to be glorified by anyone. He seemed a bad-tempered, self-important man, and he greeted Mr Fountain on the deck of his ship with a curse.

'We've missed the wind, do you realise? You and your party of children – *children*! Am I transporting a dame-school now?' He glared round at Freddie, Rose and Bella – Bella in particular, carrying an ermine muff, and with her doll Lucy dressed to match. This charming picture seemed to infuriate him, and he positively growled.

Rose put her own hand inside Bella's muff, and clasped one of the chilly little paws, drawing her back against an enormous coil of rope, out of the way of the captain's anger. She didn't quite trust Bella not to say something terribly rude, or perhaps even grow claws, like she'd seen the smaller girl do once before.

Bella shivered, looking up into the web of rigging. 'I do not like boats. Do you think we will be on this one very long?'

'It all depends on the wind,' Freddie murmured. 'And he says we've lost it. We could be stuck in the harbour for days. But it's only a few hours to Cormanse, once we get going.' He laughed, staring up at the masts. 'Faster than the journey here from London. Isn't the ship grand?'

'Oh, I cannot bear it!' Bella wailed, looking over the

side of the ship at the water. 'Look at the way it tosses up and down!'

Gus walked along the rail, his whiskers twitching disgustedly. Cats were not fond of water, he had told Rose. He was only coming on this journey because they would undoubtedly be lost without him.

Rose stared over Bella's shoulder. There was a gentle swell in the harbour, but she had a feeling that this did not count as rough weather, and that it might be rather worse when they were actually out at sea. Her stomach turned over, but she was reasonably sure that it was fright, not seasickness.

'Perhaps we should go below?' she suggested, gazing out along the side of the ship to the open water. There was such a lot of it. It was disconcerting to think that soon – she wasn't sure whether to hope for a wind or not – they would be out in the middle of it, unable even to see the land. The massive coils of anchor chain around the capstan, marked with weed and strange crustings of shellfish, seemed a lifeline, connecting them to the earth.

As it turned out, they were not long delayed, the wind rising in the right quarter the next morning. Rose sat in the little wooden bunk with her arms around Bella, who was positively shaking as the timbers groaned

beneath them. Gus was stretched out beside them, shivering, his white fur tinged with grey, and his eyes shut tight. They were sharing a cabin, and Freddie and Mr Fountain were in the cabin alongside.

'Shall we look out of the window?' Rose suggested, glancing longingly at the round, brass-framed porthole. 'It might help to see what's happening.'

When they were still at anchor she had been anxious to go below, but now she found it very odd to be moving whilst enclosed in this little wooden box. However strange it would be to see the water crashing past them, surely it would be better than airless confinement.

'No.' Bella shuddered. 'Actually, I would prefer it if you would put that blanket around my head, so as to block out the awful watery noise.'

Gus groaned in agreement. Rose sighed, and resigned herself to a long and boring journey. But some time later she realised that Bella's moans were dying away, and she was sagging back against the bedclothes. Gus had crawled under the blankets, and was now only a sullen lump. Carefully, Rose wriggled away from Bella, standing up slowly and stretching her cramped limbs. Then she crossed eagerly to the porthole.

She was only torn away from the terrifying, spellbinding sight of the solid walls of greyish-green water by the strange noises that suddenly broke out

overhead: angry shouts, scuffling and the banging of hatches. Footsteps began to race past outside her cabin, and Bella stirred, turned over, and thankfully slept on.

Rose wrapped herself in the old Macintosh cloak that had served her so well through the snowy winter, and quietly opened the cabin door, following the young midshipman who was pelting down the gangway.

He seemed surprised to see her, but was polite in helping her up the ladder to the deck.

'What is all the noise, do you know?' she ventured to ask, half-expecting him to laugh and tell her that it was some strange ritual of the sea.

'I'm not sure, Miss,' he replied, with an odd bob of his head, almost a bow.

Rose nearly fell backwards down the ladder. It was just as Bella had said. In her good dress, and Bella's laces, even swathed in that strange old cloak, they thought she was a gentlewoman.

'Should I help you across the deck, Miss?' the boy enquired, but he looked anxious.

'Oh, no. Please. You must attend to your duties.' Rose didn't want the poor boy to get into trouble with that Tartar of a captain. She caught hold of a helpful bit of wood – which probably had some important purpose, though she had no idea what – and gripped it tightly. The ship swayed underneath her like a huge animal. A sea monster, perhaps. She smiled grimly at the thought as a wave slopped over the side with a crash, the water sloshing perilously close to her best boots.

Slowly, she worked her way around the deck, holding tightly onto anything she could find. The shouting was coming from the forecastle, where she could see a group of uniformed officers, gathered around some object lying on the deck.

'Throw it overboard,' one of the men roared, and Rose was unsurprised to see that it was the captain.

'Sir, really—' another officer disagreed, but he was interrupted by a small blond fury.

'You can't! I know he's a stowaway, but I tell you, I know him! He's our kitchen boy, he must have stowed away in the hold for a lark. Sir, I promise you, just let me fetch Mr Fountain to vouch for him.'

'He will be pressed into service. Confine him below decks on ship's biscuit and water,' the captain snarled.

'No!'

Rose forgot about holding on and dashed headlong into the knot of dark coats to help Freddie fight. He was standing there with his fists raised, looking desperately small against the men, his eyes wide with panic.

Lying on the deck boards at his feet was a pitiful

figure, white with sickness, and bleeding from a cut on his face. He was completely still, and for a horrifying moment Rose thought that Bill was dead.

Dropping to her knees beside him, she pressed her hands to each side of his face, and felt him still warm under her fingers. 'What have you done?' she cried angrily, looking around at the men.

But none of them seemed in the slightest bit ashamed.

'They hit him,' Freddie told her angrily, crouching down beside her. 'The great beasts.'

'Stand away from him, young lady!' the captain ordered. 'He's a criminal.'

'He is not!' Rose wrapped her arms tightly around Bill, and felt him begin to wake out of his faint.

'He was stowed away in the hold.' One of the younger officers tried to take her arms and pull her away, but she shook him off. 'Believe me, Miss, he's not someone you should be associating with.'

'Where's the master?' Rose demanded anxiously, and Freddie stood up.

'Can you wait, if I fetch him? I didn't want to leave Bill alone before.'

Rose nodded, but one of the officers seized Freddie's arms. 'Not so fast.'

'Let *go* of me!' Freddie pulled angrily, and the man

laughed. It was probably the laugh that did it – if he hadn't laughed, Freddie would not have been quite so furious. As it was, Rose stretched out a hand, wanting to stop him, but it was too late. Freddie's eyes had turned even darker than usual, black as coals against his pale skin and white-blond hair. And then they closed, and a faintly satisfied smile curved Freddie's lips, and there was a sudden rush of air, and a crash, and the tight group of officers looming over the children was scattered as a heavy block fell from the rigging.

The young lieutenant couldn't have proved it was Freddie who made it hit him on the shoulder. No one could. But they all knew. Tearing his sleeve from the man's loosened fingers, Freddie turned away, dusting down his jacket with a look of cold amusement at their frightened eyes.

A worried whisper ran through the officers and the sailors who were gathering in the rigging. None of them followed Freddie, even when he turned and began to run for the hatchway. A few of the officers even backed away from Rose and Bill a little. Rose wasn't surprised. Sailors were known to be terribly superstitious, and that block had clearly not fallen by accident.

'Is she one as well?' she heard one of the

midshipmen whisper, and she tried to look forbidding and dangerous. But she had never felt less magical. Bill's blood was dripping onto her cloak, and the sight of it made her feel far sicker than the movement of the ship. She stayed huddled next to Bill, one arm round his shoulders, trying to pillow his head, the other hand clutching the little hanging pocket under her cloak, where her china doll was hidden.

'What is going on?'

Rose's sickness faded slightly at that lazy voice, and she turned in relief, spotting a familiar pair of pointy-toed boots through the white-trousered legs surrounding her.

'Why is my apprentice being treated like this? Rose, my dear, are you hurt?' Mr Fountain's voice was outraged, and the men fell away to let him stand next to her. 'And what has happened to this boy?'

'One of my men found him climbing out of a trunk in the hold.' The captain had not given ground, and he was glaring furiously at Mr Fountain. 'Would you like to explain why?'

'Certainly not.' Mr Fountain sounded affronted – as though explanations were beneath him. 'I can, however, confirm that he is a member of my household. I had not intended to bring him with me, but now I find he will be very useful. Clearly the standards of behaviour aboard this vessel are not what I was expecting, and my daughter and my apprentice will require a male servant for protection among such company. You.' He pointed to one of the midshipmen. 'See that he is brought to my cabin. I shall have to expend precious energy on healing him. I only hope it will not slow down my work for His Majesty. Rose, Frederick, come with me.'

EIGHT

'Has that boy woken up yet?' Freddie leaned over Rose's shoulder, peering down at Bill.

Rose shook her head. Bill had lapsed back into unconsciousness as he was carried below deck, and he was now sleeping white-faced in Freddie's bunk.'What on earth was he doing?' Freddie muttered, curling himself onto a sea chest and peering over at Bill's bandaged head. 'If he had such an ambition to go to sea, why didn't he just talk to the master? And I still don't understand how he did it.'

'Bill was in charge of bringing the trunks down from the attics,' Rose explained. 'He must have made sure there was an extra one.'

'And then barricaded himself inside it?' Freddie

sounded doubtful. It was rather extreme.

Rose sighed. Freddie would never understand. 'He doesn't have any magic, Freddie. How else could he do it?' She shivered, thinking of yesterday's long, boring coach journey, bumping over the rutted roads, as the carriage had grown colder and colder. Bill had had no fur rug, and he wouldn't have had any idea how far they had gone. Endless blackness, broken only by moments of panic when someone opened the door of the baggage coach to check that everything was still tightly lashed. 'What if someone had loaded the trunk upside down?' She gulped, feeling suddenly sick again. 'And how did he get *out*?'

'Had a knife, didn't I?' someone muttered, and Freddie and Rose swung round. Gus leaped out of a hammock to take up a position on Bill's feet.

'You are very foolish,' he told the boy sternly.

Bill stared back at him with dislike. He regarded Gus as a devil in disguise, and usually refused to acknowledge him at all. But the bang on the head seemed to have loosened his tongue.

'I'm not leaving her alone with you lot,' he slurred.

Rose stared down at him. 'You did this because of me?'

'Couldn't let you go gallivanting without anyone to look after you.'

'I would have looked after her!' Freddie protested angrily.

'Oh! No one needs to look after me, except *me*!' Rose cried.

'I'm so very glad to hear it.' Mr Fountain was seated suavely on the sea chest, gazing at Rose in amusement. 'First Gus, and now the kitchen boy. People do seem to want to protect you, Rose.'

'He's an apprentice footman,' Rose answered crossly. 'And I never asked him to come!'

'How did he get there?' Bill muttered, lifting himself up on one elbow, and wincing. 'He wasn't there before.'

'Magic, my dear William. You didn't see me arrive, that's all. You know, if you had told me you wished to go abroad, I would have gladly brought you with us.'

'Don't want to go abroad!' Bill retorted. 'Can't imagine anything worse. But you don't know what Rose's like! She walks under horses' hooves, and you can't drag her past a shop. She isn't safe out. Who knows what she'll do somewhere foreign?'

'That's not fair, that was ages ago, I'm not like that now!' Rose wailed. Bill was making her sound like an idiot.

'Like I said, sir. I've come to protect Rose. Her and me both being orphans, she's got no one else to have

a care for her. But I'll do any other duties you have for me, sir,' he added hastily.

'So far it's been me and Freddie protecting *you*,' Rose snapped. 'The captain wanted to throw you overboard! That most definitely makes up for the horse.'

'Try to be a little more gracious, Rose. You may not have wished for the boy to protect you, but he has put himself in danger for your sake.' Mr Fountain stood up. 'What I came to say was that amazingly enough, we have a strong following wind.' He coughed lightly, and looked at the ceiling. 'Most fortunate. And so we shall be landing at Cormanse in an hour, or so the only officer brave enough to speak to me seems to think.' He paused at the door and cast a rather guilty look at Rose. 'Which does mean that someone ought to see about waking Bella up…'

'I hadn't known we was going by train,' Bill muttered, wide-eyed, to Rose, as they watched the cloud of steam roll towards them out of the tunnel, eerily lit with flashes of red and white light.

'Not you as well.' Rose eyed him irritably. 'What is it about trains? I don't see that they're so very special.' She was excited too, but not about the train. They were abroad! Foreign parts looked surprisingly similar to

England, though, she had found with surprise. She wasn't quite sure what she had expected.

But the inn, where they had spent the night! Miss Bridges would have been ashamed to have such damp beds, and there had been no tea at breakfast, only coffee that was more chicory and mud than anything else, Rose had thought. If this was the great Talish Empire, she was certainly glad the channel had never frozen over, and let them come invading.

'It's only wheels,' she muttered irritably. She *missed* tea.

Bill glanced at her disgustedly, and then over her shoulder at Freddie, who shrugged. Quite clearly they agreed with each other, for once.

'Fifty miles an hour…' Freddie sighed. 'Horses can only manage fifteen, Rose. And that's a team of the very *best* horses. Oh, look…'

There was a mournful hooting sound, the clang of a bell, and the train drew out of the tunnel, gliding surprisingly smoothly for such a heavy iron beast. Freddie and Bill waved their hats in the air and cheered, and even Rose laughed at how grand it seemed. Bella was sitting on one of the trunks looking grumpy. She hadn't recovered properly from her seasickness, and constantly complained of the cold. She coughed ostentatiously as the steam swirled around her.

There was a babble of Talish voices across the platform at once, as their fellow travellers demanded that their baggage be stowed away. Railways were far better established in Talis than they were in Britain, since the emperor had taken an interest very early, realising that trains were the perfect way to carry men and weaponry to the battle-front. Now, as the Talish Empire expanded, it went by rail. The newest addition to the railway was the branch that led over the Alps, by which they were to come into Italy, following the advance of the emperor's forces.

Rose could not be as excited about trains as Freddie and Bill, but it was very gratifying to see the countryside slipping by so swiftly all that day, and to feel that every minute brought them closer to Venice.

Pine forests rattled past, and Rose smiled, thinking of the gingerbread house back at the provision merchants. Perhaps there were gingerbread palaces nestling in these woods. She leaned against the window glass, and dreamed of beds, pillowed with chocolate satins.

'Sir...' Rose turned from the window at last, and looked across the compartment to Mr Fountain, reclining thoughtfully against the overstuffed red velvet seat. 'How is it that Venice has not been brought into the Talish Empire? They have taken

Genoa, I remember it being in the newspaper.'

Mr Fountain looked thoughtfully at Bella, asleep under a grey woollen rug that a stewardess had provided. Bella and Gus seemed to share the same attitude to travelling – that it was better to sleep through it. Gus was the strange lump on Bella's legs.

'Would you like to invade a city full of Bellas, Rose?'

Rose shook her head, her eyes widening. 'Is everyone in Venice a magician then?'

Mr Fountain laughed. 'No, thank goodness, or perhaps we would be living in fear of a Venetian Empire instead of a Talish one. But the whole ruling elite are magical. And there are a lot of noble families in the city. It's teeming with magic. You'll like it, Rose. Far more of the sort of magic you want to see – practical things done by spells. The duke even has a fleet of magical ships, so I've been told, though that could just be a tale.'

Rose nodded, and leaned back in her seat, watching the trees as they raced past, mile after mile through the gathering night, to the magic city.

The train did not run all the way into Venice, Mr Fountain had explained, as they drew nearer. There was no bridge for it to run over. The city floated alone in the greenish-black lagoon, refusing to be tied down to the mainland. They would have to board another boat to cross to Venice itself, and then another to reach the palazzo of the British Ambassador. The railway line ended rather sadly, almost at the water's edge, and the huffing engine had to back away into a siding, staring out across the water and denied those last few miles.

Rose stood huddled in her cloak at the ship's prow, feeling the salt spray splash up, and squealed with delight at their first sight of the city. The glowing orange lamplights reflected in the water, the domes and bell-towers were only shadows against the stars. *Almost there...* The mask, and Gossamer, flashed into her mind, blurring the shining picture. But Rose shook her head. Gossamer might have brought them here, but she refused to think of him now.

Stepping into the strange, dark gondola for the very last part of their journey, Rose blinked drowsily at the glimmering blackness of the water. She was trying to work out what day it was. How long ago had she waved goodbye to the tall white London house, wishing that Bill had come to see her off? She smiled to see him now, squashed up at the front of the strange black boat, staring just as much as she was. A day for the carriage ride, and then sailing the next morning. The night at that horrid, dirty inn. A whole day in the train – so then it was still only the third day? Cormanse had seemed much like London, but here, they were surely more than three days from home. It felt wonderfully unfamiliar. And magical. A whole city floating on magic.

Rose gazed up at the elaborate buildings on either side of the canal, the palaces of the great Venetian families. It was late evening, but many of the buildings had lights showing, or glowing shutters pulled across their windows, and here and there a painted face shone out in the flickering light, or a jewelled mosaic pattern sparkled. It was nothing like London. The water seemed to change everything, making it shimmery and dreamlike.

Bella, who was still feeling seasick, declared that Venice smelled, but Rose thought it was no worse than the horse smell of her own city. She sighed delightedly as they rounded a bend in the canal, and swept past a palace lit with flaming torches on either side of its water-door. It was surrounded by more of the eerie black gondolas, and party guests in sumptuous satin costumes were being gracefully handed out into the torchlight. Rose's eyes widened as she noticed that many of the guests wore delicate, jewelled masks. Fiori had been right. Rose suppressed a shiver, wondering what those masks could do.

The palazzo of the British Embassy, by contrast, was

dark, and it had taken quite five minutes for a disapproving servant to unbolt the front door. Now they were inside at last, their welcome had not improved. Lord Lynton stared at them mournfully, his lank greying hair and drooping eyebrows giving him the look of a depressed wolfhound. 'The despatch arrived yesterday. And your letter. I hadn't realised that you would be with us so soon. And at such a late hour.' The tall man regarded them through his eyeglass, shuddering a little at Gus's blue and orange eyes, which made him so clearly not a normal cat.

Gus stared back balefully, his whiskers glittering. He was in an uncooperative mood as it was. He had been splashed in that rickety boat, and his dignity had not yet recovered. The romance of the journey over the inky waters had been lost on him entirely.

'I'm so sorry to put you to such inconvenience, My Lord.' Mr Fountain bowed rather haughtily.

'Oh, no, no. No trouble at all. Gives the servants something to do, I suppose. Must apologise for the state of the house, that's all. Not expecting guests. Sheets most likely damp. No flowers. Shocking.'

Rose's eyes had narrowed at the idea that this idiotic man's servants might not have enough to do without unexpected guests, but as he waved a dismissive hand around his salon, she blinked in surprise. The room looked immaculate to her, and surely she ought to know. The arched windows were draped in velvet curtains, the kind which held the dust most dreadfully, and the ornate picture frames glimmered and shone in the candlelight. The room was spotless. Even the fire irons gleamed. At a second glance though, it was a strange, mixed-up place. The walls were covered in dark patterned silk, and lined with mirrors that reflected back the light from the absurd candelabra that grew out of them in rampant glass droplets, festooned with crystal flowers. But between the enormous mirrors, the paintings were all of bored-looking horses, in the most English-looking countryside imaginable. There was a portrait of a wolfhound, too, which bore a disconcerting resemblance to the ambassador.

'Well. Tea. It is a little late, I know, but you must have tea, of course.' Lord Lynton guided them to a delicate tea table, set with an enormous silver teapot, and delicate china cups, so thin they were almost transparent. 'Do please pour.' Lord Lynton waved a bony, languid hand at Rose, and she looked round at Freddie in horror. But she supposed he was right. He didn't know she was half a servant, and she was the oldest female present, so it was quite proper for her to pour the tea. She looked at it sadly as it trickled out of the silver pot. Thin, watery stuff, nothing like Mrs Jones's strong black brew.

'You didn't by any chance bring any marmalade?' Lord Lynton gracefully ignored Rose's struggles with the enormous teapot, and let his eyeglass fall as he looked at them hopefully. 'Enderby's Orange Preserve? There's a standing order at court, or there should be. I begged them to send it out with the official papers, but a jar broke over the Shipping and Trade Treaty a few years ago, and it caused the most unfortunate upset with the duke. Strange chap, doesn't like oranges. Set us back a good couple of years, though really, the stains were hardly a problem. No one told you to bring any, then?'

'I'm afraid not.' Mr Fountain shook his head.

'Even the jam isn't the same,' the ambassador mourned. 'I don't know what they put in it. It just doesn't taste right. How can you get raspberry jam wrong? I don't understand it.'

'Perhaps they poison it. I would,' Freddie muttered to Rose, causing her to slop tea disgracefully into one of the saucers. She hastily poured it back in while no one was looking, and gave that one to Freddie. It wouldn't do him any harm. Sarah in the kitchens did that to her tea on purpose, to cool it down.

'How long have you been the British Ambassador?' Mr Fountain asked, sipping his tea, and politely

accepting a buttered scone from Rose. It was rather an odd shape.

'Eleven years...' Lord Lynton stared miserably at the cake stand, laden with decidedly foreign-looking pastries. Rose thought they looked delicious, but it was clear that the ambassador was craving seed cake, or something plain and wholesome and most definitely English.

'Still, a most interesting posting!' Mr Fountain attempted a cheerful tone, despite their host's melancholy, which was somehow made worse by the candlelight dancing over the tightly shuttered windows. It was clear that the ambassador liked to shut away all sight of the watery city outside his little castle.

'Barbaric people. Obsessed with magic and devils.'

'Devils!' Rose squeaked. No one had mentioned that.

'Quite so.' Lord Lynton peered at her through his eyeglass. 'Not at all the place for gently reared young ladies,' he added disapprovingly, inspecting her and Bella, and apparently deciding that perhaps they did fit into this category. Although he looked doubtful about Rose's boots.

Bella pinched Rose, and grinned an I-told-you-so grin, then smoothed Rose's lace collar.

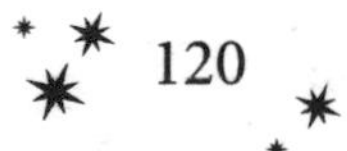

'Things rise off the water, you know,' he added. 'Glooms. Spirits. The most unhealthy fluxes. How I have survived eleven years, I couldn't say.'

Mr Fountain nodded sympathetically. 'Are you on good terms with the court, My Lord?'

Rose looked up hopefully. Would they get to the plan now? Could they confide in Lord Lynton? Perhaps he even knew where Gossamer and Venn were staying. They only knew – or hoped – that the men were somewhere in Venice.

'On such terms as I wish to be, with that gang of devil-worshipping merchantmen.' Lord Lynton rang a small bell that stood next to his chair, and stared peevishly at the door until a black-coated servant appeared, carrying a lamb's-wool wrap. 'Ah. This is Francesco. My steward. He will help you with any questions you have about the place.' His Lordship swathed himself in the woollen shawl and sighed gratefully. 'Pernicious cold. And the damp! It seeps right into my bones.'

Rose watched him from behind the teapot, her eyes wide. There was something so absurd about this most fortunate man shutting himself away in a nest of wool and marmalade, and trying desperately to create England all over again inside these clammy rooms.

*

Rose woke the next day to a strange, clear, dancing light filling the room. Her immediate reaction was to panic – if it was light, it meant she was late, and should have been downstairs lighting the family's fires an hour ago. Then she remembered where she was. In a beautifully carved wooden bed, in a grand bedroom, in the British Ambassador's palazzo, in Venice. She sighed, still only half able to believe it. Tucked in a niche of the wooden carving, the china doll smiled down at her smugly, as though it approved of the change in their circumstances. Rose wondered for a moment if she should make the doll a new dress – a prettier one, so it didn't look like a maid any more, either. She stroked the china hair lovingly.

She ran an admiring hand over the silk coverlet that was rumpled around her, and snuggled further under it. Then she realised that actually the room was warm. She wriggled up on her elbows, an unstoppable laugh rising in her chest. Someone had lit the fire in *her* room. That, more than anything else – more than the ship's officers calling her Miss, and Lord Lynton deciding she was a young lady, just about – made her realise how different things were now. A servant girl had crept into her bedroom, cleaned the grate, relaid the fire, lit it, and padded out again, all without Rose even opening one eye.

A bossy little tapping sounded from somewhere behind her embroidered bed hangings, and Rose sat up. Perhaps she was late for something, after all? But then a small door hidden in the silk-panelled wall swung open, creaking, and Bella peeped through, still in her nightgown.

'Can I come into bed with you?' She was scrambling under Rose's bedclothes before she'd even finished asking. 'It's chilly. I know Lord Lynton is rather odd, but he was right about the damp. Does this room have a balcony?'

'I haven't looked.' Rose tried to see over to the window. She had opened the shutters the previous night, but had hardly been able to see anything, only a greasy black swirl of water. But the gentle lapping sound had rocked her in her dreams.

'Mine does, but it's too cold to stand out on it yet. We're at the side of this house, but I could just see the canal. It's full of boats already, all those curly black ones.'

'Gondolas.'

There was a scratching sound at the door, and a maid peered in with a silver jug on a tray. She had obviously already tried Bella's room, as she nodded and smiled to see her, and there were two pale pink porcelain bowls next to the jug.

'What is it?' Rose whispered to Bella.

'Chocolate. But with biscuits to dip in it, too. I like being abroad.' Bella reached out for her bowl, and the maid practically purred. She kissed her hand to Bella as she backed out of the door.

'Stop bewitching everybody, Bella, it isn't fair.'

'I can't help it...' Bella turned to stare at her with huge, beseeching blue eyes, and Rose's mind felt strangely fuzzy.

'Don't!' She shook herself angrily. 'Don't you dare.'

'Well done.' Bella sniggered. 'I was trying really hard, too. You're quite as strong as me, Rose, you just don't think you are.' She sipped the drink thoughtfully, licking away her chocolate moustache with a pointed pink tongue. 'I do wonder who you are really. Magic doesn't just happen. People like us spend years planning the best sort of marriages. Almost all the magical families are related to each other somehow. Freddie is quite a rarity, as his mama is not a magician. His family was rather inbred, you see, the most awful things happened to his Uncle Menander. They had to bring in *new blood*.' Bella hissed the last words meaningfully. 'So I simply can't think how you ended up in that horrid orphanage.'

Rose shivered. The warmth of the chocolate soaking through the china bowl only made her fingers feel colder. What on earth had happened to her parents? She was beginning to think that it must have been something dreadful.

Lord Lynton did not put in an appearance at breakfast, so Mr Fountain and the children were able to discuss their plans, hushing themselves every time Francesco or the maids brought in another dish. Breakfast was the strangest combination of English and Venetian. Rose decided that she would not recommend that Mrs Jones imitated the kedgeree, which was made with something Mr Fountain thought might be octopus, instead of the usual smoked haddock. Rose mostly ate toast. She thought the raspberry jam was perfectly acceptable.

'So Lord Lynton will take us to see the duke?' Freddie asked, in a hoarse whisper.

'No one can hear you,' Gus pointed out. 'We're the only ones in the room, unless you think Gossamer has a spy concealed under the breakfast table.' He reached out a claw to hook another piece of tentacle, and gulped at it enthusiastically. It hung over his mouth at the sides like a rubbery moustache.

'Do you want mine?' Freddie muttered, watching him disgustedly.

'Later this morning.' Mr Fountain nodded,

magisterially ignoring Freddie. 'Which is helpful. It could have been tricky to get an introduction otherwise, even with the king's letters. Time-consuming, all that going through officials. Lynton says I should be able to talk to the duke directly. He thinks I'm mad of course, getting so upset about a mask.'

'Didn't you explain what it does?' Rose asked.

Mr Fountain shrugged. 'No. I just said that it was valuable, and the king wants it back. I thought the truth might send Lynton into an apoplexy. The duke is a magician, at least, and should understand how important it is. More than anyone else would, I should think. Although…' He trailed off, sighing.

'You think he might be involved?' Gus said rather thickly, through Freddie's octopus kedgeree.

'He could be. We just don't know.' He stirred his odd-coloured tea, watching it swirl. 'What perplexes me is why the duke would want to mix himself up with Gossamer at all. Why is he letting him stay in the city? And I don't see why he would allow anyone to use the stolen mask at the ritual. He must know its history, what it could do! No, there must be something we don't see. We need to tread very, very carefully. We can't just wade in and demand that the duke hands over Gossamer and the mask. What if he wants it back, for a start? There's an argument that it should never

have left the city in the first place. But I'm sure he must be aware that Gossamer is in the city. Any magician as powerful as the duke is supposed to be should have sensed Gossamer's presence.' He gave a delicate little shudder. 'I can feel the blackguard. Smell him, almost. And the mask.'

Rose nodded. She felt slightly sick, and she was sure it wasn't because of the toast. They were getting closer.

Despite being the most unfortunate choice for an ambassador, Lord Lynton was at least dutiful. As Mr Fountain had said, he attended the duke's palace every morning to exchange polite pleasantries, and flinch at all the magic, so obvious that even he couldn't ignore it. He seemed mildly horrified at the thought of taking children with him to that morning's audience with the duke, and he protested outright over Gus, but Mr Fountain waved the king's letter of introduction at him, and he subsided. From then on, Gus made a point of sitting as close to Lord Lynton as possible, and purring excessively.

'This is the Grand Canal,' Lord Lynton explained, waving a hand gloomily as they glided towards the palace in an elaborately gilded and canopied gondola, which was the official carriage of the embassy. 'The

main waterway, you know. Would make a wonderful road, if only they'd fill it in.'

Freddie snorted, and had to convert it hastily into a cough when His Lordship turned a horrified eye on him, lifting his eyeglass to examine him properly.

'You see? Coughing already. Fluxes. And the noxious gases from the water. We'll all be dead in days.'

Even Mr Fountain had to stare very carefully at the church they were passing to hide his grin.

As they approached it along the edge of the lagoon, the palace shimmered above a forest of mooring poles like a pinkish, painted cloud. Rose felt her stomach quivering as they were handed ceremoniously out of the gondola. She had been to the king's palace at home, of course, but it had been strangely disappointing. Although it looked like a wedding cake, it had a strange sense of shallow but expensive grandeur, like gold foil over wood. Rose had been sure that a palace would feel more special. This palace, oddly fortress-like above its floating arches, sent out a waft of glorious, boastful enchantment. It promised to change the life of anyone who stepped inside.

'She's most dreadfully pale. It would be unfortunate if she were to be taken ill in front of the duke. Perhaps she should wait here with Francesco?' Lord Lynton was

peering down at her anxiously, like a mournful stork.

'Oh no! No! I'm quite all right – it was only the sight of the palace… I shan't disgrace us, sir, honestly!' Rose turned away quickly to the water and pinched her cheeks to redden them up.

'Artistic child, clearly. Just watch she doesn't cast herself into the water. Is she poetic?' Lord Lynton enquired, somehow implying that poetry might be catching.

'Definitely not.' Freddie smirked.

At the top of the palace steps they were passed from servant to servant through an endless string of grander and yet still grander rooms, all gilded and painted with the most extraordinary scenes.

'Why don't the people in the paintings have more clothes on?' Rose hissed to Freddie, and clicked her fingers angrily in front of Bill's nose. He was meant to add dignity to the party, and had borrowed a livery from one of the boys at the embassy, but his gawping at the scantily clad ladies was hardly helpful.

'They're mythical,' Freddie said vaguely. 'They only wear scarves.'

Rose averted her eyes, and tried to stop Bella looking, but Bella was more interested in making sure that her best blue silk frock hadn't been crushed by their journey in the gondola. Even she gasped, though,

when they came to the audience chamber. Every inch of it was gilded or covered in the most enormous wall-paintings – even the ceiling – and the floor was tiled in extravagant patterns of inlaid marble. And at the far end of the room, raised on a set of scarlet steps, was the duke, sleepily regarding the courtiers arguing in front of him.

After the first shock of being dwarfed inside this gold and multicoloured musical box of a room, Rose looked around them as they walked slowly forward, and blinked. A good half of the people in the room were wearing masks. Either white ones that covered their whole faces, leaving only their eyes glinting strange and dark behind, or jewelled and painted half-masks, all fitted very cleverly so that they seemed almost to move with the faces beneath them.

The duke, who had no mask, but was grandly dressed in a purple velvet cloak, looked mildly interested at the entrance of the little party. He beckoned to the man next to him, who was very plainly dressed in comparison to everyone else, clearly asking him who they were.

Mr Fountain bowed graciously, but his elegant speech – which he had learned carefully from a phrase book – was ignored. The duke only had eyes for Gus, resplendent in his best topaz-studded collar, sitting

demurely by Mr Fountain's side.

There were affectionate murmurs of '*Gatto! Gatto!*' which Rose deduced must surely mean *cat*, and Gus ducked his head, and flirted his whiskers shyly, before delicately advancing up the carpeted steps to rub himself around the duke's feet.

'Charming animal!' the plainly dressed man reported gravely to Mr Fountain, and Rose realised that of course, he was an interpreter. 'He is yours?'

Mr Fountain smiled and bowed again. 'As much as ever a cat belongs to anyone, Your Grace. He is my familiar, a most talented creature.'

The duke nodded and smiled as though this was a great joke, once it had been translated for him.

Gus leaped onto the duke's lap, and purred proudly. He had obviously decided not to reveal that he could talk, which Rose thought was probably a good idea, as the duke was already patting him quite possessively. But his charming manners had the duke ordering spindly little gilded chairs to be brought for Mr Fountain and Lord Lynton, and the children ushered gently over to the windows, to gaze out on the water.

'Do you think it's going well?' Rose whispered to Freddie, casting a quick glance back over to the dais, where Mr Fountain seemed to be pleading with the duke, leaning close and gesturing sharply with his

hands. The duke stared dreamily at Gus, his cheek resting on one hand as he listened. A dark-haired man in a mask with a long, strange beak of a nose was leaning over his shoulder to listen too, and the mask made him look as though he was frowning slightly. He glanced up and caught Rose watching, and somehow the frown of the mask deepened, and Rose felt him catch at her mind, and shuddered.

A lady in a pretty feathered mask, who had been gently pointing out the names of the different islands they could see in the lagoon, smiled at her and murmured, 'That is His Grace's brother, Signor Girolamo. A very great man.'

Rose nodded, still trying to shake off the feeling of fear that Girolamo had left behind. Why did the duke's brother seem so much more alive than the ruler of the whole city?

NINE

'Did it go well, sir?' Freddie asked, as they were ushered out of the audience chamber, but Mr Fountain glared at him, and waited until they were being let out of the door of the palace, and Lord Lynton had gone off to meet another English acquaintance, before replying.

'Really, Freddie, you are the most idiotic boy. We were surrounded by servants and courtiers – did you really think I would discuss it with you there?'

Freddie looked crestfallen. 'I should think if the duke wanted to hear us here, sir, he easily could. There was so much magic in that palace, probably lots of it leaks out. There might be listening spells all over the city.'

'I wouldn't be at all surprised.' Mr Fountain sighed.

'Do you know what that building is? There, look, joined onto the palace with the strange covered bridge?'

Freddie looked over at the bridge, and the others turned to stare too. It was a delicate structure, ornamented with fanciful curls and pierced screens, and it led from the swooping arches of the palace to a squatter, hulking, grey-stained building across the narrow canal.

Freddie frowned. 'Another part of the palace? The servants' quarters? It doesn't look as grand as the other side.'

'It's dirty,' Rose agreed.

'It's a prison.'

'Next to the palace?' Rose asked doubtfully.

'For easy access.' Mr Fountain shrugged ruefully. 'What have you heard about Venice so far?'

'Just that it's full of magic. And devils, according to Lynton, but he's just soft in the head, isn't he?' Freddie sniffed scornfully.

'And it's rich,' Bella put in.

'Somehow they've managed to keep themselves out of the hands of the Talish,' Rose added. 'So it's clever magic.'

'Clever. Deceitful. Money-grubbing. Suspicious. Vengeful. You could call it all of those. But the prison

is next to the palace for when the duke takes a sudden dislike to one of his courtiers and decides to have him thrown in chains. Look. See that lion, carved into the wall of the palace? Lord Lynton was telling me about those last night. They're all over the city.' He stroked the comical little carving – the lion was cheerful-looking with a wild mane and smirking jaws. 'They connect up to the palace, all of them, with a series of tubes, and they lead to an office in the cellars, the office of the denouncements. They're for people to post accusations into, if they think their next-door neighbour is plotting against the duke. Or maybe if they themselves are, and they want to throw off suspicion.' He looked around, and waved a hand delicately in a strange pattern, making the air suddenly shift and shimmer all around them.

'What was that?' Rose reached out to see if she could touch it, and found that her fingers changed colour as she slid them through the invisible barrier. Inside, everything was a faint, bleached silver.

'A hiding spell. I need to teach it to all of you. I'm sure Freddie is right, that the whole place is carpeted in magical spies. And we mustn't use this for too long; I can't think of any surer way to attract attention. But it may be useful.'

'So, no one can see us?' Bella asked thoughtfully. She

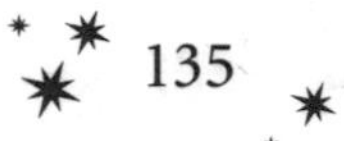

turned to look at a grand Venetian lady passing by, accompanied by a tiny shivering greyhound, who seemed to dislike the spell intensely, and stared at it with a sharp little bark. The lady sailed past, her elaborate silken gown trailing the paving stones, and seemed not to notice them at all, merely tugging her little dog away, even when Bella stuck out her tongue.

'Miss Bella!' Rose snapped, as she was sure Miss Bridges would expect her to, but actually she thought it was rather funny.

'Quite,' Bella's father murmured. 'We will learn it tonight. We must not forget lessons, after all. Frederick, do not make that face. Yes, you see, I knew you would. Strive not to be predictable, dear boy.' Mr Fountain stroked the inside of his protective spell, gently. 'I cannot guarantee our safety here. The duke was charming, but he denied all knowledge of Gossamer and Venn.' He sighed. 'Something isn't quite right. It seemed as though he hardly heard me, some of the time.'

'Did you ask him about the mask?' Freddie whispered, looking over his shoulder at the brilliant bubble of the spell.

Mr Fountain frowned. 'No. No, I had meant to, of course, but somehow, it didn't seem the right time…' He shook his head, as though shaking off a dream.

'Sir, the duke's brother…' Rose paused, unsure what to say. *I didn't like him* seemed too silly.

Mr Fountain gave her a sharp look. 'You saw it too? I had wondered if it was only the effect of that foul mask.'

'It felt almost as if he was stronger than the duke,' Rose suggested hesitantly.

The master nodded, his eyes half-closed. 'I shall have to go back, see if I can untangle it a little more. This place is like a spider's web, and if we tug on the wrong strand of silver silk, the fanged creature will be coming to kill us.' He looked round at their horrified faces, and smiled, rather hollowly. 'I don't mean to frighten you. But you have to understand. This place makes me feel like a young student again – a wonderful feeling, but terrifying, too. The stones are steeped in power, and I wouldn't be surprised if the water's contaminated. Such a strange, alien magic. It's all tied up with the duke, and his ancestors. As though his family were made out of the dust of the city, and the waters run in their blood. I don't understand it.' He rested one hand against the palace wall. 'And it feels as if the buildings are alive,' he whispered.

Rose looked around at the shining stone of the palace, and the glimmers of red brick and marble reflected in the deep and swirling waters further down

the canal. She was sure he was right. The city reminded her of her first days in the Fountain house, when she had felt the walls seething and bulging with magic, and the stairs had swooped and twisted under her.

Mr Fountain smiled, and snatched at the air with his hand to break up the spell. 'But one very good thing came of my little chat – it was Gus's doing, I think – the duke took a particular fancy to him. I have been officially invited to Sunday's masquerade, and the duke suggested that I should bring the *charming children* as well, by which I assume he meant all of you.' Mr Fountain raised his eyebrows at them.

'The masquerade? You mean, the ritual?' Rose whispered. 'We're going to it?'

Mr Fountain nodded. 'Gossamer will have to show himself then, if he wants the ritual to help him control the mask. Please God, we will have found him before Sunday, but if not, the masquerade will be our final chance.' He shook himself, and added, as though he were promising a great treat, 'I have been told we must all have costumes, and most especially masks.'

Rose shuddered. 'Must we?'

Mr Fountain stared down at her in surprise. 'I would have thought a new dress would be a good thing?'

Rose looked around, to see if anyone was listening – she

couldn't help it, even though it was probably useless. 'It isn't the dress. I don't like those masks. There were so many people in the palace wearing them, and they make my skin crawl, sir. They must be wood, or, I don't know, paper perhaps, but they moved! I'm sure they did. The duke's brother, Girolamo, I saw his mask frown. I don't want to think about what he looked like underneath,' she added in a whisper. She remembered Fiori's book, and his strange, nightmarish ideas about the magic-laden masks.

Gus rubbed himself around her legs. 'I didn't like him either. Slippery, slimy sort of fellow. Not so devoted to his dear brother, either, I'd be ready to swear.'

Rose crouched down to stroke him gratefully. She had hoped she wasn't being feeble.

Mr Fountain was frowning. 'Still, I'm afraid we must. Obviously we must be there. If we can't find Gossamer before then, it's the one place we're sure he'll be. I shall be most interested to see the ritual, anyway, and the custom is to wear masks. Lord Lynton has told me of a little shop – we are to go back to Francesco and ask him to take us to the Alley of the Bleeding Windows.' He shrugged. 'Well, that is what he said – surely it must have some strange explanation…'

*

The mask-maker was sitting at a long table, surrounded by pots of paint, brushes, and piles of glaring white masks, in hundreds of shapes. Finished masks hung from the walls in shining rows, gleaming with varnish, and twitching strangely in the water-light.

'Oh, look! A little mouse!' Bella pointed delightedly, but the mask-maker sprang up and snatched it from her reaching fingers, pouring out mouthfuls of tangled Venetian, and patting her cheek affectionately. Bella turned in confusion to Francesco who spoke a little English.

'He says no, little miss is not a mouse.' Francesco smirked. Even after a day, Bella's character was well known in the embassy.

The mask-maker seized Bella's hand, and walked with her around the walls, humming to himself and clicking his tongue. 'Ah-hah!' He lifted a mask down from the wall, and held it out to her, smiling and nodding to show she must try it on. It was a double mask, the sun on one side of the face, and the moon on the other, both exquisitely painted and smiling.

'The light and the dark.' Gus stared fixedly at the mask-maker. 'He is clever, this one.'

Luckily Bella admired the gold and silver paint, and was flattered by the pretty pink cheeks and rosy mouth of the sun side, and readily agreed for it to be hers, once it had been restrung to fit her. With similar speed, the mask-maker chose a widely-smiling mask for Mr Fountain, a bear's face for Bill, and for Freddie a face that frowned over a hooked nose like Mr Punch.

Rose had been hanging back, almost pressing herself into a display of cloaks, until the mask-maker beckoned her forward. His hands on her face were warm, and though there was a low hum of magic in his fingers, it did not feel dangerous, merely questing.

At last, though, he shook his head, and waved towards his table, holding up two fingers.

'He says he doesn't have the right one. He will have to make it special for you,' Francesco explained. 'He says come back in two days.'

Rose nodded reluctantly. However pretty the masks were, they still made her shiver.

Worn out by learning the hiding spell, and feeling strangely transparent, as if she hadn't brought all of herself back, Rose took the amazing luxury of a sleep after their lunch. They had been served the most English boiled mutton she had ever tasted, though accompanied with Venetian side dishes, such as artichokes and more strange fishy things.

She hadn't been able to bring herself to actually go to bed, but had instead curled up in her clothes on the

horse-hair stuffed sofa in her room. She woke to find Bella sitting next to her, shaking her shoulder.

'Oh, do wake up! Rose! What is the point of staying penned inside this gloomy house. I want to go and explore!'

Rose sat up, stupid with sleep, and swallowing massive yawns. 'Where is everyone else?'

'All sleeping too. It's such a waste. Please come with me, I don't want to go far, just for a little walk along the quayside, to see everything. Francesco said it's carnival time, this week before the masquerade. There might be all sorts of pretty things to see. Please?'

It was the addition of please that made Rose shake off the last remnants of sleep, and fetch her best cloak. Bella wasn't given to asking nicely, and Rose had some strange instinct that she ought to be rewarded for it.

The whole house seemed to be sleeping, and indeed, as they let themselves out of the front door, the whole city seemed quiet, with only a few gondolas poling slowly past, their men leaning lazily on the oars.

'Does everybody nap here?' Bella asked disgustedly.

'Perhaps it's the magic,' Rose suggested, staring round at the light mists floating across the water. It was already growing grey, the January afternoon drawing in. 'Maybe they're too worn out not to.'

Bella sniffed, but as they paced down the quayside

she turned to look down one of the many little alleyways, and squealed with delight. 'Oh, look! Do let's go and see!'

Floating in a stately manner along the canal at the end of the alleyway was a richly decorated barge, half-covered in flowers, and with masked girls sitting all over it, chatting and laughing to each other, and eating little cakes.

Bella pelted off down the alley, and Rose dashed after her. But by the time they reached the little stone ledge at the other end, and Rose had seized Bella, who was leaning perilously out over the water, the barge had disappeared round a bend. It left only a smell of rose petals, and a lingering dance tune from the band sitting on top of the flowers.

They wandered sadly back to their quayside, admiring the odd little shrines dotting the sides of the houses, and were within sight of the Grand Canal, when there was a strange sort of scuffling behind. They turned to see a gang of boys – quite small boys – creeping along at their heels. It would have been funny more than frightening, except that they were all masked.

'Run!' Rose seized Bella's arm and dragged her along, and Bella ran gasping, but her little heeled boots weren't made for chases, not over rutted cobbles, and

she kept slipping. At last Rose pulled her close and turned round, glaring at the boys, who had several times come close enough to grab at her cloak. She hugged Bella tightly to her side, and pushed her other hand into the little hanging pocket where she kept the doll version of herself. Holding the china Rose made her feel braver. She stared at their dark eyes, glinting through the slits in their masks. They were all animals, she realised, a sick, sour taste rising in her mouth. Ugly, brownish creatures – rats, and a fox, and a cat who was nothing like her darling Gus.

The thought of Gus brought her voice back.

'What? What do you want? We haven't any money. Leave us alone!' She knew they couldn't understand her, but it felt better than being silent.

The boys crept closer, their masks eerie, all the more so for being battered and dirty instead of gorgeously painted. It looked like they lived in them. *People who never take them off,* Rose thought, her heart beating in sickening thuds. *What do they look like underneath?* Horrible images of blackened, rotted flesh crept unbidden into her mind.

'Oh, Rose, Rose, they've got knives and I'm too frightened to scream!' Bella whispered, clutching Rose's cloak around her too.

The knives were held in front now, shining and

vicious, and Rose closed her eyes for a second in fierce concentration, summoning her picture magic.

The blades were at once covered in shimmering visions, and Rose shuddered, seeing what she had created. She hadn't meant them to drip with blood, but perhaps that was what the metal remembered. She hoped it was only from hunting rats, and nothing larger.

Two of the boys screamed, and flung their knives down, haring off back down the alley, but there were still three left, and one of them, the ringleader, only smiled at his bleeding blade – indeed he looked as if he rather liked it. He stepped even closer, waving the blade like a weaving snake's head in front of Rose and Bella, and laughing, the noise so much worse coming from under his pointed fox mask.

Rose thought frantically through the spells she had learned so quickly at the king's palace, when she was being trained as the princess's bodyguard. But she had no firelight to fling at them, and the crumbling grey stones were so much more theirs than hers that she couldn't think how to use them. At last she seized on the mist insinuating itself in wisps along the darkening alley, and cast it as ghost streamers swooping around the boys' faces. Then she ran again, hauling Bella with her.

They were almost at the mouth of the alley when Rose felt one of them grab at her cloak again, and this time she simply turned and hit out at him angrily, seizing the side of his ugly mask and pulling.

'I shall report you to the British Ambassador!' she screamed. 'And the duke. You shan't hide behind that horrible mask!' And she tried to tear it off, wrenching at it with her nails under the side. But the boy howled in agony, dropping his knife and raising his hands to scrabble her away, and then dropped back, still crying.

Rose fell back against the wall, shuddering in disgust, and Bella leaned over her anxiously. 'Rose, what is it? They've gone, you sent him running.'

'It wasn't a mask,' was all Rose could whisper. 'It was fixed. It was grown on, Bella. I was trying to tear away his face.'

'Girls!' It was an English voice, and Rose lifted her head. 'Are you all right? Did those young ruffians hurt you? Is she fainting?' she added to Bella.

'No, no, I'm not.' Rose levered herself away from the wall, her limbs shaking, and looked over to the mouth of the alleyway, where an elderly lady was signalling them from her gondola. She began to climb out, carefully leaning on her umbrella, and hurried towards them, trailing long black silk skirts. She was dressed in a rather outdated fashion, with a lace fichu and mittens, and a little cap under her bonnet. But there was something about her that made Bella curtsey very promptly, and even Rose managed to bob her shaky knees.

'I'm sorry to disturb you, ma'am, we're quite all right,' she stammered.

'You most certainly are not,' the old lady stated. 'Come and sit down in my gondola, it's quite comfortable, and I have some butterscotch. Clearly you need something.' She leaned down to peer short-sightedly at something on the ground. 'Did you drop that paper, dears? Is it something important?'

Bella picked it up. 'No. I don't think so— Oh, Rose! It's you!' She held it out, her eyes like circles.

Rose swayed again, and the old lady put a hand on her elbow, and steered her to the gondola. 'Sit down, child.'

'It is. They were carrying a drawing of me…' Rose whispered, as she sat down under the canopy. It was a very comfortable gondola, with mauve cushions, and there was a bag of knitting next to the old lady's seat.

'This is really most interesting.' The old lady tweaked the drawing out of Bella's hand. 'Yes, most definitely it's you. Do you have any idea why?' She was staring at Rose now, and frowning, looking from her to the drawing and back again as though something was itching at her.

'No!'

'It's Gossamer, it must be,' Bella suggested, and Rose tried to hush her. Surely they shouldn't be talking about him, even in front of this sweet old lady.

But the sweet old lady sat up ramrod straight and glared at Bella. 'Gossamer! That felon! What have you two to do with him?' Then she peered even more closely at Rose, frowning. 'Are you *that* child? Fountain's protégée? The one who rescued the little princess?'

Rose only nodded, but Bella smiled smugly. 'Yes, she is, and I helped her.'

'Then is Aloysius Fountain in Venice?'

'You know my father?' Bella asked, sounding unsure if this was a good thing or not.

'Fountain's child, and Fountain's apprentice…' The old lady eyed them disapprovingly. 'You are a pair of very silly little girls. What are you doing wandering round this city, of all places, without anyone to protect you?'

'Not a little girl,' Bella muttered crossly, but Rose was too sure that the old lady was right to object.

'It was just a short walk,' she excused herself limply.

'Don't,' the old lady snapped. 'Take a gondola, and guards. Clearly someone is looking for you already, and it's likely that little Miss Fountain is right – Gossamer is on your trail. That foul man. I had suspected… The city has seemed darker, these last few weeks, and colder, but I had hoped it was only my imagination…' She looked up sharply. 'Does anyone know you're here?'

'We went to the palace…'

'The whole of Venice, then. Really, Aloysius has no sense.'

'Are you a magician too, ma'am?' Rose asked politely.

The old lady looked at her sharply, and nodded. 'Indeed. I suppose you haven't met a great many lady magicians. My name is Miss Hepzibah Fell.'

Bill and Freddie were waiting outside the embassy for them as Miss Fell's gondola pulled up with a showy swirl. The boys ran over to the gondola, both looking furious.

'Where have you been?' Freddie snapped.

'We looked all over the house!' Bill yelled at Rose. 'I never thought you'd be as stupid as to go out without us!'

Miss Fell chuckled. 'I see you do have guards, after all. Tell your father I shall pay a call on him very soon, dear.'

The boys dragged Rose and Bella out of the gondola, and Miss Fell spoke to her gondolier in what sounded like fluent Venetian, and waved her umbrella at them as she sailed away.

'What's that?' Bill asked Bella, staring suspiciously at the piece of paper.

She held it out reluctantly. 'Some boys chased us, and they dropped it.'

Bill cursed quite graphically, and Bella gave him an admiring look. 'Don't you repeat any of that!' he snapped at her. 'Someone's after you, Rosie. Didn't take 'em long.'

'What on earth would they want Rose for?' Freddie muttered, taking the drawing and scowling at the real thing.

Bella suddenly seized the drawing from Freddie. 'Don't you see, Rose? I hadn't realised until now, but look!' She pointed at the drawing.

'It's Rose.' Freddie rolled his eyes. 'We know it is, Bella, keep up!'

'The paper, idiot!' Bella twisted the thick, creamy paper and at last the others saw what she meant. Woven into the threads of the paper was a faint silvery shimmer. 'You see? Gossamer! His mark!'

She was right. The paper was scattered with tiny silver snowflakes.

Freddie snatched the drawing back, his face worried. 'Already? That was quick.'

'They knew we were coming, remember,' Rose reminded him, as she trailed up the steps to the front door. 'The master said they saw him. And that he was still angry about what happened at the palace.'

'Why you, and not all of us?' Freddie sounded quite insulted.

'She was the one that bested him, wasn't she? He wants his revenge.' Bill shoved a chair at Rose as they tiptoed into one of the golden salons. 'Sit down, before you keel over, do. What happened to you?'

Rose sank onto it wearily, and let Bella tell the others about the masked boys, while she sat shivering.

'I don't like this place.' Bill was pacing round the room, occasionally kicking at table legs, and muttering. 'Too wet and too slippery, all of it. I got lost trying to find the necessary last night – it's like a rabbit warren below stairs, all these nasty damp cellars everywhere, and odd little doors all over the place. And I swear, half of them lead straight onto the water! Like there's rivers flowing through the middle of the house, secret ones. The whole city's full of nasty little dark secrets.'

'All hidden in masks,' Rose giggled, and then she looked up as Bill leaned over her. 'Don't slap me!'

'Stop that laughing then!' Bill glared at her. 'Now's

not the time for getting all missish and hysterical, Rose.'

Privately Rose felt that she ought to be allowed a mild fit of hysterics after being set upon by a gang of masked ruffians, but Bill was eyeing the vase of flowers on the nearest table, and she knew he'd pour it over her head if she argued.

'I'm not hysterical. But don't you see? That boy's mask was part of him. It has to be because of this ritual. I wish we knew what they actually do. How can they make masks stick to people's faces? It's all wrong.' She stared round at them anxiously. 'We can't let Gossamer be there for the ritual. If he ends up stuck to that mask, no one will ever be able to stop him.'

TEN

Mr Fountain was furious when Bella and Freddie dragged Rose up to his room, but not with them.

'Lies, all of it,' he snapped. 'All that sweet chatter. Every word the duke said. He pretended he'd never even heard of Gossamer. I cannot believe that from someone so tied to the magic of the city – and that's what it is, he's woven into it. I can feel him at the centre of it all, as though his bloodline holds it all together. I simply refuse to believe he didn't know as soon as Gossamer arrived. Or at least as soon as he started employing gangs of little Venetian ruffians!'

'What will you do?' Rose asked. She still felt trembly.

'I shall go back there, tomorrow.' Mr Fountain

scowled, his moustache quivering. 'As a representative of the British Crown. And I shall ask His Grace just what he thinks he's doing, allowing Gossamer to go around kidnapping people.'

'I don't think His Grace can do anything more than smile and nibble sugared almonds.' Gus strolled along the back of an elegant, narrow sofa, and Mr Fountain sat down next to him, as though his legs had given way.

'That bad?' Mr Fountain sank his head in his hands. 'Why ever didn't you say so before?'

Gus laid his ears back slightly. 'I was considering. And it was a very powerful spell. Extremely well hidden. I had to think about it.'

'You were enjoying the fuss he made of you so much you couldn't think straight.' Freddie smirked, and Gus's tail twitched angrily. Then he sighed.

'True. I should have seen it at the time.'

'Was it the brother? Girolamo? He made my skin crawl, but I don't know if that means it was him...' Rose shivered.

Mr Fountain smiled wearily at her. 'I don't know, Rose. But you should go and lie down. Get them to bring you supper in bed, child. And Bella, stay with her.'

Gus rubbed his chin against his master's shoulder, and then jerked his head at the door. It was obviously a dismissal, and Freddie helped Rose up, and beckoned Bill and Bella after him.

Mr Fountain appeared at breakfast the next morning – kippers and crumpets, and tea that Lord Lynton sighed over disgustedly – looking positively confident, and Rose watched him worriedly. Did he know what was going on at the palace, or was it all an act? Freddie had sworn to her that half of what made their master such a brilliant magician was his ability to make people think what he wanted them to.

'Gus was right. There must be an enchantment on the duke. I need to go and test it further. See if I can work out who laid it on the poor man, and when. I shan't take you with me.' Mr Fountain crunched his toast delicately. 'No, not you either, Gus. Too much of a distraction. Stay in the house,' he warned them. 'Especially you, Rose. After what happened yesterday, we can't risk anything. I'm afraid Gossamer must have his people watching the house.'

Gus draped himself protectively over Rose's shoulders, like a furry white scarf, and nipped her ear. 'I shan't let her go anywhere.'

But even Gus was pacing irritably by that evening. They had spent the whole day cooped up, arguing with each other. Rose had gone so far as to hurl the travelling

chessboard at Freddie's head, after he patronisingly tried to explain the rules to her *just one more time.*

'Well, it's plain to see you've forgotten all about being in service,' he snarled nastily, and Rose flinched. It was true. A good servant would never even have thought of such a thing.

'Shut up, Freddie. She isn't a servant.' Bella put an arm around Rose's shoulders. 'You like her being an apprentice when it means her sharing the work, but then you fling that in her face. It's cruel!'

'She's always a servant when you want your hair curling!'

'Stop sniping at each other!' Gus came stalking back to them from the window, his tail lashing to and fro. 'Something's wrong. Why is he not back? He cannot still be closeted with the duke, I refuse to believe it. He should be back.'

'You don't think – a long meeting? There was so much to talk about, with the mask... They might even have gone off to find Gossamer,' Rose suggested.

'The duke would not spend all this time with one envoy. And Aloysius would have sent for us, if it was to be a chase. Or for me, at least.' Gus ran his claws into the silk carpet in frustration. 'They've got him,' he spat bitterly. 'We let him walk off into a trap. I should never have let him go alone.'

Lord Lynton, when they interrupted him in his study, was not helpful. He regarded them as mere children – and an animal. He paid no mind to their magic, and merely suggested that Mr Fountain might have met with some acquaintance.

'He would have sent a message, though, surely.' Rose was staring into the prettily framed mirror in her room, trying desperately to see something, anything. But she could only see herself.

'Of course he would!' Freddie was gazing anxiously out of the window at the small stretch of canal he could see. He was trying to sound brave – he was the oldest after all, or claimed he was, and it was hard for Rose and Bill to argue – but he was turning something over and over in his fingers, as though he couldn't bear to be still. It took Rose a few turns to realise that it was the marble he had made in Miss Sparrow's cellar, all those months ago. The soft light glowed through his fingers. Freddie saw Rose watching him, and slid the marble swiftly into his pocket. 'Lynton's an idiot. Do you think we should go after him?'

'Not in the dark.'

The children turned to look at Gus in surprise. Usually, he had a cat's natural love of night-time prowling.

'Not here.' Gus jumped up onto the dressing table, and put his front paws against the elaborate glass-flower mirror frame, so he could see into it too. He flicked his whiskers irritably as nothing more than a plump white cat appeared in the mirror. 'Not even a hint of him. Gossamer's magic is too strong. Have you noticed that it's snowing?'

Freddie flung the window open, hanging out to see. Rose stared across the room, shivering in the sudden cold, and saw that Gus was right.

Silently they watched the flakes twirling lazily down. They were cruelly clear in the light of the lamp, shining from the wall on the other side of the canal.

'It could just be snow,' Bella whispered, but she didn't sound as though she believed it.

'It isn't. I can feel him in it,' Gus hissed.

'Sorry,' Rose whispered, and he stood on his hind legs to rub his face against hers.

'It isn't your fault, dear Rose. We couldn't see him last time either. And his magic is so powerful here. I can't understand how Gossamer caught Aloysius again – we were so careful! He was laden with protective spells!'

'But Gossamer has the mask now,' Rose reminded him sadly. 'It's making him stronger already.' And Gus laid his paws on her shoulder, resting his head there for a moment, as though he couldn't bear to think of it.

That was when Rose began to be very, very frightened.

When Mr Fountain had still not reappeared the next morning, Lord Lynton agreed, somewhat reluctantly, to take Rose, Freddie and Bella to the palace with him. They could think of nothing else to do, and the palace was at least the last place they knew Mr Fountain had been. Surely the duke would have to talk to them?

Bill followed them out of the embassy, dutifully carrying Lord Lynton's cloak, in case he should want it, and the ambassador didn't send him away. Indeed, he looked at Bill thoughtfully – it seemed the servants he had originally brought from England had liked Venice even less than he had, and they had all gone home years ago.

But as they approached the huge audience chamber through the chains of interlocking rooms, Lord Lynton was pounced upon by a masked courtier, who led him away, talking very earnestly about who knew what.

The children stood gaping after them as they hurried away, and Bella sat down with a flounce on a gilded chair. 'Whatever that man just said was all a lie, I swear. Someone just wanted to distract Lynton from asking

anything difficult, and get rid of us. What are we to do now?'

A pair of courtiers entered the room, deep in conversation, almost arguing, they thought. Freddie stepped forward politely to ask where they should go, but the men simply veered round him, and disappeared out of the far door.

'They're pretending we're not here.' Rose went over to the window and peered out, trying to see where in the palace they actually were. Not that it made much difference, but she had to do something, or scream. Suddenly, she turned back from the blurred glass, smiling enough to show her teeth. 'I feel quite worried. We've been most rudely abandoned in the middle of the palace, and we have simply no idea at all where we are. I feel as though I ought to go and look for someone to help us, don't you, Freddie?'

'Rose, stop play-acting! Whatever's the matter with you?' Freddie scowled at her, and went back to staring at the door in the hope that someone might walk through it.

'Oh!' Bella gasped. 'Oh, yes, Rose. I think we should. I think we should look *all over the palace*!'

Gus purred lovingly at them, so much so that Rose could see his sides shaking, and Bill chuckled. At last,

even Freddie's eyes widened, and he stared at Rose in surprise. 'Oh, I see! Yes.' He nodded frantically. 'Only because we don't know what else to do, of course.' He looked all round the corners of the room, as though the listening spells might gather there, and nibbled on his thumbnail. 'There really isn't anything else we can do…' he added to the ceiling, as they scuttled out of the room.

They felt so much like spies and conspirators that it was almost galling when the hurrying courtiers took no notice of them, even when Rose flattened herself against the wall every time anyone went by.

'Stop that!' Gus hissed. 'You look dreadfully guilty. Just walk. And for heaven's sake smile.'

'Where are we actually going?' Bill demanded, ten minutes later, as they came into yet another room, this one full of portraits of staring dukes.

'Well, I don't know, do I?' Rose glared at him. 'Somewhere. Anywhere's better than spending the day waiting for them to bother to notice us. He could still be here, hidden away. He might be in the very next room, as far as we know!' She flung out an arm dramatically, pointing at the door at the end of the gallery. Then she stopped, staring.

'Look!' Gus bounded forward, his whiskers bristling, and Rose gasped. 'It's them! Should we chase them?'

'They've seen us.' Freddie had already started running.

At the end of the long, windowed gallery stood a man in a mask – a strange one, with a long, beaked nose. Girolamo, the duke's brother.

But it was the men with him that had set Freddie and Gus and the others racing down the gallery, even though they had no idea what would happen if they caught them.

Chatting idly with the second-most powerful man in Venice was Gossamer, a pale mask dangling from his fingers, and beside him, in a strange, golden chair, was his accomplice, Lord Venn.

It was Venn who saw them coming, and now he was tugging at the skirt of Gossamer's coat, and mouthing something strangled. As she ran closer, Rose saw with horrified fascination that he could not speak. She was not even completely sure that he could move any more than his fingers. His chair was like the wicker bath chairs used by invalids at watering places, but this one was all metal, with a glossy golden finish. Even that wouldn't have made it so very strange. The problem was that it was hard to see where the chair ended and Lord Venn began.

Images flashed in front of Rose's eyes, of the little golden bird that Venn had presented to her when they

met before, a living creature encased in metal. It seemed a terribly fitting punishment that Lord Venn should have shared the bird's fate.

Gossamer looked up at last, and smiled, a triumphant, knowing smile, and with insulting slowness he waved his companions through a door at the end of the gallery. Girolamo stepped out obediently, like a trained dog. Venn's chair glided like a gondola after him, smooth on greased wheels. Rose shuddered when Lord Venn's dreadful rolling eyes caught her own as she raced the last few steps to catch them. He looked desperate.

And the door swung shut with a satisfied little click.

'What *was* that thing?' Freddie asked, as they sat leaning against the door, panting.

The door had remained obstinately closed, however hard they rattled the handle, and even after Freddie and Bill tried to charge it, and fell over each other.

'It was nasty.' Bella shook herself. 'It was part of him – like that boy's mask, Rose,' she added – reluctantly, as if she didn't want to remind her.

'How did it move?' Rose asked. She was huddled close between Bella and Bill, and Gus was sitting on her lap, leaving hairs on her good cloak, she noted wearily.

Freddie shrugged. 'Magic. I don't know which spell. Something linked to his mind, I suppose. I don't think he could move for himself.'

Gus snorted. 'I'm not sure he had much mind left, either. He was half-dead when you poured your power into him before.'

'Rose did for him good and proper.' Bill sounded smug, but Rose gave him a horrified look.

'You think I wanted him to be like that?'

'Better like that than running around kidnapping princesses, I reckon.' Bill shrugged. 'Looked to me like that Signor Girolamo is hand-in-glove with Gossamer now.'

The door opened suddenly, making Bella squeal, and a scandalised lady-in-waiting peered down at them – four children and a cat, sitting on the best oriental carpet.

They scrambled up, and Freddie tried to explain that they were looking for Signor Girolamo, but she refused to listen. Instead she escorted them back to the room where they'd been left, bristling with disapproval.

Lord Lynton blinked at them through his eyeglass, as though he'd almost forgotten they were with him. 'Oh. Where did you get to? Do come along, the duke has sent the most interesting proposition about the trade treaty, and I must go and draft a dispatch at once.'

'But, what about Papa?' Bella asked, catching Lord Lynton's hand, and staring up at him in confusion. 'What did the duke say about Papa?'

'Oh, yes.' Lord Lynton blinked again, and frowned. Then he nodded happily, and a strange slow tone came into his voice. 'I didn't see the duke himself, but I spoke to several of the most influential courtiers. Apparently the duke was very surprised to hear that your father had not returned – they met yesterday, and Fountain left the audience room after an hour. Don't worry, my dear. I'm sure he's just busy,' the ambassador told her vaguely, tucking her hand in his arm, and walking on like a benevolent grandfather out for an excursion. 'Signor Girolamo mentioned that they had a most interesting conversation yesterday. He was quite complimentary.'

Rose's eyes widened at the mention of the duke's brother, and Bella was about to argue, when Freddie shook his head. 'No point. Can't you tell? He's been spelled. Made to forget, somehow. He won't even hear you talking about it.' He sighed. 'Look how cheerful he is. It's not like him at all. It must have been when he was talking to Girolamo.'

It was true that Lord Lynton had lost his mournful, homesick air. He practically chortled as he sauntered down the palace steps towards the quayside.

'I don't mind spying around the palace when the other side are going to enchant the British Ambassador,' Rose muttered. 'I suppose if Lord Venn can't even speak, he isn't a great deal of use as an accomplice. Bill's right. Gossamer's using Girolamo instead.'

Gus picked his way down the steps delicately. 'I should think Signor Girolamo would do anything for a magician who told him he could take his brother's place. I shouldn't think it's all that exciting to be only the brother of a duke.'

'He's going to replace the duke with Girolamo?' Rose nearly fell down the steps.

'I doubt it...' Gus sniggered, and stared up at her. 'But he probably told Girolamo he would.'

'We should warn the duke,' Freddie said anxiously.

Gus nodded, his eyes wide and shining. 'Of course! Because it was so easy to get in and talk to him just now. And we can lift the enchantment on him without the slightest difficulty.' He stared out across the lagoon, his tail twitching with scorn.

Freddie scowled. 'Well, what do you think we should do, then?' he snapped. 'Come on, Lynton's calling us.'

Lord Lynton was beckoning them over to the gondola. 'Have you picked up your masks for the ball yet?' he asked hospitably, as they clambered aboard.

Freddie shook his head. 'No, sir. He did say today, but with Mr Fountain not here...'

'Oh, stuff!' Lord Lynton waved this away. 'You must be ready for tomorrow night, all of you.'

'Surely we can't go to the ball without Mr Fountain,' Rose began, but Bill hushed her.

'Now isn't the time for company manners, Rosie. And them masks might be useful,' he whispered. 'Disguise, see.'

Freddie gnawed his lower lip, and nodded, but Rose couldn't bear to think of putting on one of those masks. She wondered how many of the servants and courtiers they'd seen today had been able to take theirs off.

Was it something special about the boy's mask? Had the ugly brown fox mask done that to him, or was it something he himself had done? And how many others had done it too? It had to be linked to the ceremony at the heart of the masked ball.

The mask-maker's shop looked welcoming, with a light burning through the tiny windows on such a dull day, and glimmering in the water that ran beneath them. Rose still had to force herself to step inside.

The mask-maker sprang up, clearly delighted to see them, and he handed Bill a large box to carry. Rose made a move to go, but the man swooped round in front of her, and shooed her, chattering the whole time, into sitting in a little black chair in the centre of the shop. Rose looked around twitchily, realising that she had been placed as the star of the show, and the others were gathered as an audience, eagerly – jealously, in Bella's case – watching.

With a triumphant twirl, his tattered apron swinging, the mask-maker brought out a delicate little mask. It was a half-mask, painted a soft silver, and edged with glittering gems. At least, they looked like gems. Rose was sure they were only paste, but she didn't care in the least. She had never seen anything so pretty, much less owned it. She reached out a hand, and stroked one of the jewels with a loving finger. She wanted desperately to put it on, but she couldn't help remembering the boy in the alleyway, and the courtiers at the palace, whose masks had looked skin-tight and so very comfortable.

The mask-maker's voice took on a wheedling tone, and he pressed the mask into Rose's hands so that he could reach something swathed in a calico bag on the wall. He uncovered it with a flourish, shrugging and gesturing apologetically. It was a dress, made from some sort of rich brocade, woven in shades of violet on a blue background, and covered with a misting overskirt of cobweb silver lace. Rose blinked, dazed with longing, and Lord Lynton gave a disapproving sniff.

'He says that his sister is a dressmaker, and she saw the mask, and happened to have some stuff which would match it, so she has made you this, Miss Isabella having mentioned when you were here before that you were in need of a dress. You are under no obligation to pay the man for it, Miss Rose. He is taking a liberty, and I daresay the dress is an unwanted commission, and they are very glad to be rid of it.'

Rose hardly heard. In that dress, wearing that exquisite mask, who would ever believe she had so much as seen the inside of an orphanage? She would look like the most petted, adored little miss. She would be a lady. She wanted it.

She had forgotten her dread of masks. In this one, she was sure, she would be the real Rose.

'Sir, Mr Fountain did leave some gold with you, did he not?' she whispered. 'I do not have a dress for the ball, and he wanted me to buy one here. Do you think you could pay the man, if he sent a bill?'

Lord Lynton shrugged. 'Oh, very well. It is tolerably pretty, I suppose.'

The mask-maker bristled at his dismissive tone, even if he didn't understand the words, but Rose patted his hand, and smiled gratefully at him. Then

she picked up the mask, enjoying the rough feel of the gems under her fingers. She could feel them sparkling, and they sent a little thrill of happiness fizzing into her blood.

It was cleverly made, with a place to put a stick to hold it by, but he had fitted it now with long silver ribbons to tie around her head. Rose closed her eyes as she lifted it in both hands, feeling the soft silken ribbons weave themselves lovingly, perfectly, around her fingers. The mask seemed to jump in her hands, as though it was desperate to be worn, and Rose brought it up to her face with a glad little sigh, settling it on the bridge of her nose – oh, it fitted so well, like a second skin—

Then suddenly it was snatched away. Rose screamed, in shock and anger, and gazed up at the mask-maker, her eyes blurred with tears. How could he do this? It was her mask! He had said so. He had made it for her. He couldn't take it away!

But he was shaking it at her, his black eyes snapping, and a stream of furious Venetian pouring from his mouth.

'What is it? What is he saying?' she demanded of Lord Lynton, half-sobbing. Bella had flung her arms around her, and Bill was hovering by her chair, fists clenched.

The ambassador shook his head in disgust. 'These fellows are all full of superstitious nonsense. He says, would you believe, that he will not sell you the mask, if you are so eager to put it on. He says that if you wear it with your heart open, as it was' – here Lord Lynton rolled his eyes – 'then the mask will grow into your heart, and one day you will no longer be able to take it off.'

ELEVEN

'But you must go, my dears.'

Miss Fell was sitting bolt upright on Lord Lynton's striped silk sofa, eyeing Rose, Bella and Freddie with surprised disapproval. She had arrived that morning to find Lord Lynton still unusually cheerful, and Gus and the children rapidly running out of hope. 'If Aloysius has disappeared – which frankly doesn't surprise me in the least, he always was the most careless and lackadaisical child – then you cannot pass up such a wonderful opportunity to find him.'

'You knew Papa when he was little?' Bella asked, fascinated.

'Of course.' Miss Fell raised one narrow arched eyebrow. 'I must be your cousin, some several times removed. Certainly we are related in some way.'

'Oh.' Bella eyed her a little anxiously. Miss Fell looked like the very worst kind of relative – far too observant, and a stickler for good manners. Except in the case of gatecrashing masked balls, evidently.

'Miss Fell…' Rose hesitated. Should they tell her about the mask? Miss Fell already knew about Gossamer and the princess, but Mr Fountain and the king had been so anxious to avoid a panic with the news of the mask. Rose eyed the little old lady, her hands in their lace mittens neatly folded on the silver head of her stick. She did not look like the sort of person who panicked.

'What is it, child?'

'It isn't only Gossamer. Or rather, it is, but…'

'Don't mumble, dear. Come to the point.'

'He stole something from the king's palace, when he was in London. A mask, one that came from here a long time ago.'

Miss Fell's piercing blue eyes fixed on Rose, and she leaned forward, her sharp nose giving her a sudden hawk-like look. 'You mean Gossamer has the magician's mask?'

'Ye-ees…' Rose wilted under Miss Fell's glare.

'Good gracious. How on earth did Aloysius let that happen?'

'It wasn't Papa's fault,' Bella said sulkily.

Miss Fell gave Bella a very aunt-like look, and Bella shut her mouth with a snap. 'This puts a different complexion on things,' Miss Fell murmured. 'I had been relying on you children to retrieve Aloysius yourselves – you seem perfectly capable, and I do not go about in company a great deal these days, it's simply too tiring.'

Rose exchanged a glance with Freddie. Miss Fell looked to them like one of those indestructible little old ladies who goes on for ever, bullying generations of her distant relatives.

'Really, why Aloysius had to go meddling at the palace, I just don't understand. But then he always was an inquisitive little boy.'

'We were worried that the duke had been bewitched,' Gus told her bluntly, only the twitch in his tail betraying how worried he really was. 'He seemed…clouded. And then when we went to look for him yesterday, we saw Gossamer with the duke's brother, Girolamo…'

Miss Fell's delicately arched brows drew together. 'Venetian history is full of the most shocking family feuds. But could Gossamer really…? Well, that settles it. I shall have to tell Maria to get out my heliotrope silk. The duke always invites me to this ridiculous affair, but usually I decline. But if Gossamer is going to be messing about with masks, I shall make the effort. I will be quite prostrated for the next week, of course, but there. I cannot go searching through the palace, like you young things, but there are other ways I can help. And I shall most certainly speak to His Grace.'

The children stared at her doubtfully, but Miss Fell gave a small, sly smile. 'Old ladies have their uses. They won't dare refuse me an audience, my dears.'

'But I still don't see how we can go at all! The invitation for tonight was to Mr Fountain,' Rose protested. 'How can we just arrive at a palace ball without him?'

'Rose, you must try not to be excessively worried over trifles. You are Lord Lynton's guests, you can very well go with him.' Miss Fell glared at Rose severely, and then she sighed, and gazed thoughtfully at the ceiling, as if she were trying to think what to say. 'My dear, the duke's parties have a – reputation. There will be a great many people milling about, and by the end of the evening, many of them will be somewhat the worse for wear.' She closed her eyes in distaste. 'No one will notice you combing the palace for Aloysius, you will just have to be careful not to trip over the sleeping revellers in the passageways.'

Rose raised her eyebrows – it did not sound like a duke's party to her. 'How very odd.'

Bella made a strange little noise in her throat, looking from Miss Fell to Rose and back again.

'What is it?' Rose frowned at her.

'Nothing. At least – no, nothing…' But she was frowning at Miss Fell as she said it.

Miss Fell smiled back at her, another strange, complicitous little smile. 'Hmm. Yes, quite so, Bella dear.' Her sharp blue eyes flicked back to Rose. 'A most marked resemblance,' she murmured softly.

Rose was about to ask her to explain, when the old lady suddenly shook her head, and was all briskness again. 'Even if it were a dreadful thing to do, needs must, Rose my dear. Aloysius must be in that great prison-hulk of a palace somewhere. You will never have a better time to search for him.' Then she closed her eyes for a second. 'It pains me to say this, but I must. If Gossamer has the mask, then he will surely be at the palace tonight, and you will have to stop him taking part in the ritual. Somehow. He cannot be there at midnight. That is even more important than finding Aloysius.'

Bella gasped, and Gus let out a tiny hiss. Freddie stared at Miss Fell, wide-eyed with shock.

Rose swallowed painfully. Three days ago, after the

boys had attacked her and Bella, she had said herself that Gossamer couldn't be allowed to use the mask in the ceremony. But she had never thought it would come to a choice between stopping Gossamer and finding Mr Fountain.

Miss Fell nodded, and said gently, 'You know that it's true. Of course I devoutly hope that you *will* rescue Aloysius, and then you will all deal with Gossamer together. But it may not be that way, and you cannot let Gossamer become even stronger. That man, and that mask…' She sank back against the sofa cushions, suddenly looking very, very old. 'I have seen the ritual before, and I know what it can do. Only for a very few of those there, but…'

'So what exactly *does* it do?' Gus growled. 'I'm tired of hearing stories about it.'

Miss Fell's voice was thin and whispery. 'It does what it was always meant to do. It strengthens the magic in the city. It shows the duke's love for his people. But – it's very strong magic. Old magic that's been built up over the centuries, and sometimes it works too well. The more you wear a mask, and the more you love it, the harder it is to take it off. The ceremony makes it even more so. It can bind the mask and the wearer together, if they want it. It strengthens any magic the person already has, and it seals the spells that are on the mask into their skin.'

'I thought so. That's why they don't come off?' Rose whispered faintly. 'That boy's mask had grown onto his face.'

'I don't see why anyone would want to do that.' Freddie was frowning. 'Aren't most people here magicians anyway? It sounds horrible. Why would you want to wear a mask all the time?'

Miss Fell smiled. 'Venice is a city of secrets, Frederick. Some people only want to show a painted face.'

Rose gave a nervous little gulp, and then burst out, 'The mask-maker we went to didn't want to let me take my mask. He said I wanted it too much, and if I put it on when I felt like that, one day I'd never be able to take it off. He let me have it but I had to promise him I'd never put it on because I wanted to be someone else. Does that make me a terrible person? Like Gossamer?'

Miss Fell reached out a hand and gently stroked Rose's cheek. The lace was scratchy, and smelled of lavender, and Rose shivered. 'Rose, if you were like Gossamer, you would have snatched the mask, and left the man dying in his shop. There is nothing wrong with wanting to pretend a little, here and there. But the man was right. You must be proud of who you are.'

Rose sighed. That would be easier, if she actually knew who she was.

'Miss Fell, why doesn't the duke just stop the ritual?' Bella asked. 'If it makes people dangerous?'

'Stop a ritual that's been passed down for centuries?' Miss Fell raised her eyebrows. 'There would be a revolution. It isn't only the people in the palace, you know. He goes out to the piazza, and the whole city takes part. Besides, not everyone who is truly masked becomes dangerous. People simply become more – themselves.' She sighed. 'Or who they think they are. Which is why you cannot let Gossamer be there.' She eyed Rose thoughtfully. 'You need to take care, my dear. He has already sent those boys after you, and after you fought them off so easily he may decide to attack you himself.'

Rose blinked. It hadn't seemed easy at the time. She could still remember the awful feel of the boy's mask as she'd tried to tear it off.

Miss Fell leaned closer, staring at the little silk pocket hanging from the waistband of Rose's dress. 'You already have some sort of protection, don't you? Did Aloysius cast it?' She frowned. 'Whatever it is, it's very strong...'

Rose gazed at her blankly. She had no idea what the old lady was talking about.

'The doll!' Bella chirped proudly. 'She means my doll. Well, it's hers,' she explained to Miss Fell, 'but I gave it to her. For Christmas.'

Slowly, almost reluctantly, Rose drew out the little porcelain creature, and Miss Fell smiled admiringly. 'All your own magic.'

'It was an accident,' Rose admitted. 'She got mixed up in a spell, and I cut myself.'

'Accidental spells are often the strongest. So it was a gift… And you keep it with you all the time?' she asked sharply.

Rose nodded.

Miss Fell stretched out one finger, and stroked the shining brown-painted hair. Then she shook her head. 'Look after her, Rose. I can't give you anything stronger than your own little poppet.' She stood up to leave, but then she hesitated, leaning heavily on her stick, as though she were feeling her age. 'Rose. Did I hear the news right in my letters from home, that you came into apprenticeship with Aloysius by accident?'

Rose flinched. That was only a roundabout way to ask if it was true that Mr Fountain had dragged her out of an orphanage. But she nodded politely.

'And you are not sure who your real family are?'

Rose smiled. It was a kind way of putting it – to suggest that her family were somewhere, waiting for

her to come back to them. 'I have no idea, ma'am,' she replied quietly, refusing to be ashamed. Miss Fell had said she should be proud, and she would be. It was not her fault they had abandoned her, after all, at least she didn't think it could be. Mr Fountain had assured her that she would have looked like a perfectly normal baby. But all the teasing in the kitchens had left its mark, and she had nursed Susan's taunts about changeling children made of wax and hair-clippings far too close inside.

Miss Fell stood staring at Rose, as though she were measuring every line of her face.

Rose tried not to feel self-conscious, but at last she could bear it no longer, and burst out, 'Is there something wrong, ma'am?'

'Not at all,' Miss Fell snapped briskly, and eyed them all with a critical frown. 'You have suitable clothes for tonight?'

Rose couldn't help but smile at the thought of her dress, even with the way things were, it made her glow inside to think of wearing it.

She didn't see the stricken look that flashed across Miss Fell's eyes as she caught Rose's smile. But Bella did, and she turned to look at Rose again, frowning a little.

Miss Fell nodded. 'Good.' She hesitated, for just a

second. 'You will all be careful?' she asked quietly. 'I know you defeated Gossamer once before, but the man is clearly willing to do anything. Stay together.' She looked round at Freddie and Bill and Bella, and there was a pleading tone in her voice. Her last words were only under her breath, and Rose hardly heard them. 'Please take care of her. So cruel to lose her again…'

That couldn't be what the old lady had said – it made no sense – but Miss Fell was hobbling surprisingly fast to the door of the Gold Saloon, and Bill was showing her out.

Gus sneezed crossly. 'You notice she still didn't tell us what this dratted ritual is?'

The quayside around the duke's palace was so thronged with gondolas, and even one amazingly gilded barge, that the little party was forced to disembark some way from the entrance. But this was no hardship. The waterside was busy with little knots of guests in the most elaborate clothes, laughing and showing off their costumes, and they spilled over into the huge square in front of the cathedral. Crowds huddled around the edges of the square, the people of the city in just masks and cloaks over their everyday things, admiring the richer costumes of the aristocrats.

Several children darted about between the crowds,

and Rose flinched as a boy in a mask flitted past her. But it wasn't the boy from the alleyway, just a child playing tag with his friends.

Bill laid his hand on her arm. 'You're shaking.'

Rose turned to him, smiling apologetically beneath her mask. Her eyes glittered like the gems that surrounded it, and Bill stared. 'You look more like a magician than ever with that thing on,' he muttered. 'Suits you though, I suppose.'

'It frightens me,' she whispered back, leaning against him to breathe into his ear. 'Because I love it so. What if I start to love it too much, like the mask-maker said? If I want to wear it always, like Miss Fell told us?' She was silent a moment. 'Bill, if you think it's becoming part of me, will you promise to take it off? Even if – even if you have to tear it away?'

Bill shifted uncomfortably. 'Not if it means tearing your face, like you said with that boy. How could I? Besides,' he added in a husky whisper, 'you look pretty in it.'

'I'd rather be dead than not be anything underneath it.' But Rose was blushing behind the plaster mask.

'It's cold out here,' Bella complained. 'Can't we go in?' They had not brought cloaks, Lord Lynton explaining that the party would be a sad crush, and there would be nowhere to leave them. But there was

a sharp wind blowing off the water. Rose was warmer than everyone else, as Gus was draped around her shoulders. He had glamoured himself flatter, so that he looked like a little fur tippet.

Lord Lynton, who had been admiring the dresses through his eyeglass, nodded and led them through the crowds to the palace entrance.

The marble-floored rooms that had seemed so huge were now not large enough for the crowds swirling and sparkling inside them. Branches of candles burned everywhere, and in the main ballroom hung an enormous chandelier, dripping with crystal droplets and golden glass flowers, the candles making stamens of living flame. The light reflected on the dancers' silken skirts, and the satin coats of the men.

'Oh,' Rose breathed in delight, and then she gave herself a little shake. She must not forget that they were here to find Mr Fountain, who was most probably being kept shut up by Girolamo and Gossamer in some horrible dungeon over that strange crooked bridge. She was not here to dance, even though her feet itched to join the spinning patterns on the dance floor.

Lord Lynton had disappeared into the throng, and Rose could not see Miss Fell anywhere. But then, if there really were as many people here as there seemed to be, they might never see her all night.

'Oh, I can't just stand here!' Bella cricd. 'We can't go searching yet, not while everyone's still being polite.' She seized Freddie's hand, and ran with him into the gathering crowd. 'Smile, Freddie, let's dance.'

Rose sighed, watching them, and looked hopefully at Bill, but he shook his head firmly. 'Manservant, remember? Like as not, they'd have me drowned for dancing. Find a gentleman, Rosie. That's what you need now.'

'I can't just ask some stranger to dance!' That would probably be more shocking than dancing with Bill. But it did look such fun.

A draft blew in from the doorway, and the candles guttered for a moment. Rose shivered, and patted her shoulder in confusion. Where had her pretty fur gone?

She was staring at her sleeves, and hardly noticed when someone came to stand in front of her. Someone with warm, soft skin, who took her hand.

Rose looked up, and swallowed. Standing before her, dressed all in white, even down to slender white fur slippers, was a tall and handsome boy. He was masked, but his mask was made of glittering ice-white fur, and had the pointed ears of a cat. Silver wire made the whiskers, and it had diamond chips for teeth. The mask was half-covered by the hood of a short white fur cloak. It was a most effective costume, and several of the other guests were murmuring admiringly.

The boy bowed low to Rose, and held out one white-gloved hand in an unmistakeable invitation to dance. As she stared up at him, Rose noticed that the boy had one deep blue eye, and the other was a strange shade of tawny gold. And his tongue was pink and sharp and pointed, as he flicked it across his lips.

'Gus?' she whispered, as he whirled her into the dance. 'You're a boy? I didn't know you could do that!'

'You didn't know I can skin a rat with my whiskers.' Gus shrugged elegantly. 'I can do a lot of things. And we may as well enjoy ourselves. We will only look suspicious if we lurk about being miserable.' He smiled, the whiskers of the mask twitching. 'Besides, I can smell the supper table. There is a lot of lobster, and I do not want to have to skulk under the table to eat it.'

Rose smiled, and closed her eyes as he spun her round and round the dance floor. It would be far too easy to forget their mission and simply keep on dancing.

The dancing had changed now – no more decorous pattern dances, but riotous, romping waltzes, the women's skirts flaring out in a flurry of silk as their partners whirled them round the floor.

Rose stood watching by a delicate silver tree, a slender sapling that seemed to be made of living metal, its leaves adding a shimmering bell chime to the music. Little jewelled birds sung on its branches, but they were not real inside. She had checked, after the first horrified moment, when she had felt sick at the sight of them. Although that might have had something to do with the lobster, as she and Gus had eaten rather a lot of it, and she had followed it with ices.

Freddie and Bella appeared suddenly in front of her, spat out of the swirling dance, and stumbling slightly.

'Still no sign of Gossamer?' Bella murmured.

Rose shook her head. She had been looking so carefully at all the masks, searching for that strange mushroom-pale one she'd seen hanging from Gossamer's hand. But most of the dancers had bright, beautifully painted creations.

'It's time, don't you think? Late enough to go looking?' Freddie asked. 'Where are Gus and Bill?'

'In the supper room. Bill thought no one would be in a fit state to mind, and Gus found they had been keeping back some lobsters. He says boys have bigger stomachs than cats, and he's making the most of it.'

Gus sighed dramatically when they appeared, and eyed the half-dismembered lobster in front of him regretfully. 'I suppose you want me to leave this behind?' Standing up, with one hand protectively over his stomach, he ducked under the tablecloth. Freddie made to look underneath, but Bella pulled him back. The tablecloth billowed, and there was a prolonged and unpleasant retching sound, then Gus appeared, wriggling out from beneath the linen, and looking very small.

'Are you all right?' Rose asked, and he nodded, briskly licking a paw and sweeping it over his ears.

'Oh, yes. Don't worry. It was quite worth it. Where shall we start?'

'Miss Fell was right.' Rose gazed disgustedly after a party of revellers, who were reeling down the passageway. 'They practically collapsed on us.'

'Wait a minute! Did their masks look different to you?' Bill stared after them as they staggered around the corner. 'Sort of tighter?'

Bella nodded, giving Rose a slightly anxious look. 'Don't faint, Rose. But I think he's right – those were the kind that don't come off. They wrinkle like skin.'

Rose was frowning after them. 'When we first came to see the duke, Girolamo had a group of people around him, and I'm sure they all had the masks that don't come off. I remember that black-and-white diamond one, I'm almost sure...'

'You think that lot are working for Jerry-whatsit?' Bill asked. 'And Gossamer?'

'It's as good a clue as any,' Freddie agreed. 'We haven't found anything suspicious so far, and it feels like we've been over half the palace.'

Rose nodded, swallowing carefully. 'They came up that flight of stairs over there.'

They moved over to the stairway, already starting to move in a cautious creeping sort of way, as if it would help.

'Do you think this palace has eyes?' Bella suddenly murmured, as they walked slowly down the stairs.

Rose and Freddie glared at her, and Bill sniffed. Gus, who was leaping ahead, hissed. 'Don't even suggest it. How do you know it won't take a fancy to the idea?'

Bella stared around her at the dark wood of the stairs. There were little faces carved among the garlands of leaves that swagged the banister, monkeys grinning with sharp teeth, foxes, a sly-eyed cat. It would take very little imagination for them to turn and follow the children as they went on down the steps. Mr Fountain's house was full of odd quirks like that, so the palace was bound to be.

'Stop thinking about it!' Gus snapped at them, which was of course impossible. 'Or at least go faster. There are no more of these dratted carvings once we

get off the stairs, and I shouldn't think they can uproot themselves, horrible little things.'

The little wooden cat stretched and stared after him malevolently.

'Move!'

They skittered down the rest of the steps, their party finery swishing around them, and cannoned off the stairs into a flagged passageway, hung with tapestries. It smelled old, and the flagstones were worn smooth with thousands of footsteps.

'Is this an ancient part of the palace?' Rose whispered. She wasn't sure she believed in ghosts, but if they were going to be anywhere, it would be here.

The passageway was long, and the doors that occasionally led off it all seemed to be locked. Most of the keyholes were ornate metal ones, snarling lion-faces, with very obvious teeth. Gus sniffed one, and shuddered. 'Put the wrong key in, and it would have your hand off, I think.'

After that everyone drew into the middle of the passage, as far away from the doors as possible.

'Is it just me, or does this passageway slope downwards?' Freddie asked a while later. 'It's been going on for ages. We must get somewhere soon.'

'I wouldn't bet on it,' Bill muttered, but then he rubbed his hands over his arms. 'It's getting colder, too. And damp.' He pointed to the wall – the tapestries had run out some time ago, and there were dark, greenish streaks on the stone. 'I reckon we're heading for one of those underground canals, like at the embassy. Perhaps they all link up?'

'Come and see!' Gus had padded round a corner, and now they found themselves at an abrupt dead end, facing a solid-looking wooden door. In the middle, an even larger lion's head held a massive iron ring in its mouth. The lion was smiling, in an inviting sort of way.

Rose and the others turned to look at Gus, who was sitting in front of the door looking small and thoughtful. 'This is the water door. I can feel the stream flowing on the other side. And hear it. Just a quiet ripple, nothing more.'

'I hope that's not the kind of lion that bites fingers off,' Rose said warily. 'It looks quite friendly, and it isn't as if we can put the wrong key in, you only have to turn the ring.' She looked hopefully at Gus, remembering his abilities with door handles, but he shook his head.

'That won't work here.'

'There's some marks on the wood,' Bill pointed out, crouching down to look. 'Um. They *could* be blood...'

Gus managed an expressive feline shrug. 'They *could* be anything.'

'I bet it only bites human fingers,' Freddie suggested. 'Could you swing on the ring?'

Gus gave him a disdainful look. 'I am not a trained monkey from the circus.' Then his ears twitched suddenly, and the fur rose up along his spine. 'There's someone coming!'

Freddie looked back along the corridor. 'No, there isn't.'

'From the other side!'

They hustled back around the corner. 'Is it just one person?' Freddie demanded.

'Sssh!' Gus stood listening, his eyes closed, whiskers trembling. 'Yes,' he said at last.

'We could hide ourselves, with that spell Papa taught us,' Bella suggested.

'But then the door would still be closed.' Rose took a deep breath. 'If we grab whoever's coming, before they shut the door, then we could get to the water. I'm sure we're close to your father, Bella.'

'What if it's Gossamer coming?' Freddie whispered.

'Then we're all dead, I should think.' Gus shrugged again. 'Stay here.' As he strolled back round the corner, they could see him changing, his aristocratic white coat shading, till he became a striped brown tabby, its ribs showing through the rippled fur.

Rose peeped round the edge of the wall, and saw him

sitting in front of the door, looking like the most unmagical alley cat, admittedly a very lost one. Then her heart thudded in panic as she saw the ring in the lion's mouth start to turn, and she whipped back round the corner, flattening herself against the wall.

The door creaked – of course it would, Rose thought, listening to it groan, and trying not to shiver – and someone stepped through.

Gus mewed plaintively, and a surprised voice answered him – a boy's voice, not Gossamer then.

Rose looked round at the others questioningly, and Freddic nodded. She was just readying herself to run round the corner, when the boy's voice rose into a sudden howl of terror, and Freddie shoved her sideways and shot past her.

The boy was lying on the flagstones in front of the door, and Gus was standing on his chest. He was no longer any sort of cat, but rather a huge mastiff dog, although he had kept the tabby coat. His sleek brindled fur covered hulking shoulders, and he growled in the boy's masked face with enormous, slavering jaws.

'Oh.' Freddie sounded rather disappointed. 'I don't think he needs any help at all.'

'Did you want to be heroic?' Bella giggled.

Freddie went red, and Rose patted his arm. At least

he had tried – she had still been summoning up the courage to move.

'What are we going to do with him?' Bill stared down at the boy. 'If we let him go, he'll tell the whole palace, like as not.'

'We could drop him in the river.' Gus nosed at the boy's ear thoughtfully, and then growled as the boy yelled in terror.

Rose crouched down and looked at him. Something about that yell had sounded familiar. She stood up quickly, feeling sick at the sight of the battered fox mask. 'That's the boy from the alleyway.'

'Really?' Bella squeaked, inspecting him. 'Yes, you're right. He works for Gossamer. Oh, surely this must be where Papa is!'

The boy had clearly recognised Rose's voice, for he snarled something unintelligible and spat on the floor. Gus set up a low, steady growl, so deep it made the floor shake, and the boy shook too, muttering what sounded like most heartfelt prayers.

'There's a boat in here,' Bill suggested, looking back from the doorway. 'And some spare rope. I say we tie him up and dump him in the boat. We can untie him when we come back.'

No one said *if*, but there was a strange little silence as everyone thought it.

In the end they gagged him with Bella's sash, too, as he was very inclined to shout. Then they set off in single file down the narrow bank of the underground stream, led by Gus, his white fur shining in the thick darkness. It was lucky that Freddie still had the strange glowing marble he had made in Miss Sparrow's cellar, all those months ago. But it was still mostly dark, and the water was so horribly close. Rose could feel it sucking at the side of the bank, almost as though it was waiting for her to overbalance and fall in.

Suddenly it was even darker, as Gus mewed loudly and bounded further ahead.

'Is it Papa?' Bella gasped, and tried to run forward, sending Rose lurching perilously close to the water.

'Oh! Oh, help!' She teetered on the edge until Bill hauled her back, and grinned. 'You owe me again. See. Told you that you needed me along.'

'No-o-o!' An unearthly wail rose ahead of them, and they stumbled anxiously along the path, almost falling over Bella and Gus. Bella was crouched by her father's side, chafing his hand. Mr Fountain lay on his back, sprawled across the path, the other hand almost trailing in the water. As Freddie lifted the glowing marble above them, its light caught on the silver hilt of a knife, dug deep into his chest.

TWELVE

'I'm sorry... You must have been so worried...' Mr Fountain's voice was a painful whisper.

'Why didn't you come back?' Bella scolded him, but her voice was wobbling.

'I saw Gossamer, you see.'

'We saw him, too.' Rose kneeled down by his side, hardly able to look at the wound – the knife had plunged in so deeply, it looked wrong.

'I followed him – down here...but then he slipped away...there are so many tunnels and streams, I was lost before I realised it. The magic down here? Can you feel it? This part of the palace is so old, it does have a life of its own, and it seems to deaden my magic, as though it senses that it's foreign. I couldn't use it to find my way out, and I couldn't send you a message. I had to just keep trying all the different paths. Gossamer has the mask, of course, so the magic doesn't try to stop him...' He wheezed to a stop, gasping for air.

'We saw Gossamer with Signor Girolamo, yesterday. We came looking for you, but the duke said you had gone.' Freddie was staring at the knife, his fingers twitching as though he wanted to pull it out. Rose put her hand on his.

'Don't pull it,' Bill muttered. 'He'll bleed to death...' He looked apologetically at Bella, but she only nodded, her eyes so wide they seemed to fill her face.

'We were right,' Mr Fountain wheezed. 'He is under a spell. But I couldn't get close enough even to see what it was. No...private audiences. Gossamer's got him.'

'We saw Lord Venn, too,' Rose whispered. 'In a horrible sort of chair that stuck to him like those masks.'

Mr Fountain laughed, painfully. 'Not any more. Venn is dead.' He lifted a hand, trying to point, but he couldn't raise his arm. 'Along there, somewhere. I'd worked my way back as far as this door, so close, but then Gossamer came back. With Venn – in that foul chair. How he ever got him down here, I don't know, but I think he needed Venn's magic to draw on. It was still there, however little else of him was...'

'You killed him?' Rose whispered. She and Freddie had once set a strange spirit on the evil Miss Sparrow, and she supposed they'd known it would kill her. But they hadn't actually touched her, or so Rose had always told herself, as though that made it better. Venn was – had been – a murderer, and a kidnapper – but still. It was hard to think of Mr Fountain killing people. She *knew* him – he was ridiculously fussy about his moustache, and liked Lancashire cheese. He didn't kill people.

'I was trying to kill Gossamer. But they were linked, he was pulling Venn's magic out of him, using him up. And the spell stopped Venn's heart, I think. He was very weak.'

'And then Gossamer did this to you?' Bella let out a hate-filled breath.

Mr Fountain nodded, his hand groping blindly for the knife. 'It's got a spell. See the snowflakes on the hilt? It's icing me up, from the inside. I can hardly feel my fingers.'

'We have to pull it out!' Bella reached for it, but Bill grabbed her. She wriggled in his arms, fighting and biting, and then opened her mouth to scream.

'Don't!' Rose yelped. 'Bella, we still don't know where Gossamer is. Do you want to bring him down on us? Don't scream!'

Bill shook her. 'You want to kill him quicker?' He growled it in her face, and she glared back at him with dazed, angry eyes. 'Whatever spell it's got on it, it don't change a knife that much! He's still going to bleed to death if you pull it out!'

'What can we do?' Rose looked at him hopefully, but Bill only shrugged.

'Magic? He's got no hope, else. That's deep. It won't stitch. It's in his vitals.'

'Sir, how did Gossamer stab you?' Freddie sounded confused. 'I would have thought...'

'You are very kind, Frederick, to think I can't be beaten... But yes, for the sake of my pride – he had the mask, you see. After he'd used up the power he was drawing from Venn, he put it on. He hadn't wanted a straight fight, he hoped to catch me unawares down here.'

'He's using the mask?' Rose's heart seemed to race, and she stumbled over her words as she tried to explain. 'Sir, Miss Fell told us that tonight's ceremony will bind him and the mask together, and she said we mustn't let that happen. But – but we don't know what strange spells are on that mask already. What if he doesn't even need the ceremony? What can he do, if he has the mask on?'

Mr Fountain sighed. He sounded even weaker than

he had a few moments before. 'Who knows? This is why we had to chase him all the way here. We have no idea what it can do… Except that on him, it will be nothing good…' Mr Fountain seemed to rally slightly. 'Gossamer didn't want to put it on, Rose. I could see it in his eyes, as he was holding it. He doesn't know how to control it, and he's frightened of what it might make him do.' He pawed helplessly at the knife again, and there was a thread of frustrated anger in his voice. 'So stupid of me! We must stop him! Now, before the ritual makes the mask a part of him, and we can never get it away. If only I hadn't let him taunt me. It worked… He's clever, the devil…'

'Taunt you? What could he taunt you about?' Rose frowned. 'We beat him last time!'

'You, Rose. All of you. You and Freddie, and my little Bella…'

Bella tightened her grip on his hand, and he smiled faintly at her.

'He told me he'd taken you all. Even you, Gus. I didn't know whether to believe him or not. I hesitated, lost concentration for a moment – and he stabbed me to the heart.'

Rose stood up, fury burning inside her. Gossamer was doing it again. Using Mr Fountain's love for them, the same way he had counted on England's love for

Princess Jane. 'I'm going to stop him. I'll kill him, if I have to.' She shuddered at the thought, remembering how shocked she had been, only a few moments before, at the idea of killing someone. But surely Gossamer deserved it…

'You won't.' Gus had walked away from Mr Fountain, and was now sitting at the water's edge, staring into the gleaming blackness. 'Because I will.' His yowling voice echoed eerily across the water. He turned back to look at her, and purred, very quietly. 'But you may come with me, if you like.'

'No!' Mr Fountain struggled to sit up, but Bella scolded him in loving whispers, and he sank back again. 'You can't. It's too dangerous.'

'I will not be distracted.' Gus's voice was proud. 'Rose and I can defeat him, Aloysius. He's already weakened from the fight with you. He can't control the mask properly. Now is the time! It must be almost midnight, he'll be waiting with everyone else upstairs. We must fight him now, before the ceremony makes him and the mask even stronger. We would be fools not to.' He prowled back to stand beside his master, his whiskers tickling Mr Fountain's cheek. 'Old friend, you know I would never leave you otherwise.'

'Don't talk like that,' Bella hissed. 'He isn't dying!'

But everyone knew that he was. And Mr Fountain

sighed, letting his hands fall back to the ground, as though he was letting go, letting them go. 'He stood over me, laughing. He's been out there watching us, all this time. He has a ship, you know, out on the lagoon. But close in. We would have been able to see it, from outside the palace, if it hadn't been for the mask. The city's magic worked to hide its own creature. A ship with black sails…'

Rose sniffed. 'That's just showing off. A real magician wouldn't need to make that sort of fuss. I feel better about fighting him, now I know he'd do something stupid like that.' She looked over at Freddie. 'Will you stay here with him? And Bella?'

Freddie glanced quickly at the little girl, and Rose nodded, a movement so tiny Bella wouldn't notice it. Freddie knew what she meant. When her father died, Bella was going to be distraught, and Bella, with her magic just starting to grow, might be almost as dangerous as Gossamer.

'I'm coming with you.' Bill stood up.

Rose shook her head. 'You can't! You won't—' She couldn't say what she wanted to say, which was that he wouldn't be any use. She couldn't say something so cruel. But she wanted to, desperately.

'I'm coming,' he told her again, glaring, and Rose gave in. Bill might not have any magic in him, but he was clever, in a cunning sort of way, much more so than she was. They might need cunning. And she had a feeling that Bill was more ruthless than she was, too.

'All right.'

'We should go now.' Gus's tail was flicking back and forth in excitement. 'The longer we wait, the more time Gossamer will have to recover from his fight with Aloysius.' And he was off, running along the bank with the speed of someone who could see in the dark.

Rose and Bill followed by the gleam of his coat, and every so often he would double back to round them up.

The dancers in the hall were still going as they sped swiftly past, searching for Gossamer.

'Look for Girolamo, too,' Gus hissed. 'He's in league with Gossamer, poor fool, they'll be together.'

'Wait!'

Rose stopped, and a few seconds later, Gus came back, his tail swishing furiously now. 'Why are you wasting time? We're in a hurry! We have to find them!'

Bill gave him a dirty look, which Gus returned hard enough to make Bill take a step back. 'Don't do that! Look!' He pointed out into the middle of the dance floor, where a couple were twirling gracefully, swooping and spinning and adding in odd courtly little bows to each other. The woman was a tiny, beautiful

creature with red hair, and a primrose-yellow dress – and the masked man was Gossamer.

'Is that the mask?' Rose's mouth felt swollen, she could hardly get the words out. It was white like so many of the others, but this was a strange shade of white, an absence of colour, which seemed to suck the brightness out of everything around it. Gossamer's face looked oddly pale already. The mask fitted him horribly well, transforming the upper part of his face into a bleached, horned creature with strange hollow eyes. Or perhaps his eyes were like that on their own?

Gus nodded. His whiskers were bristling with hate. 'Yes. That is it. He has killed my master, and now he's dancing.'

'Well, he's crazy, isn't he? We know *that*,' Bill muttered uncomfortably. He couldn't stand Gus, but no one could hear that coldly miserable voice and not have sympathy.

'Gus, come back!' Rose hissed. The white cat was walking in a straight, determined line across the dance floor, and strangely all the drunken couples still managed to avoid him. Gus didn't come back, and Rose moaned in fear, and followed him. The spell, or whatever it was, did not extend to her. A very fat man in a strange white-faced mask with tears painted on it nearly trod on her foot, and someone else kicked her.

Gossamer had seen them coming, she realised. There was a strange glitch in the music, as though half a dance tune had suddenly been played very fast, and then everyone was suddenly bowing and curtseying all around her, and Gossamer was leading his partner swiftly across the floor back to her chaperone.

Gus veered after him, carving a strange channel through the dancers, as Gossamer made for the door, and Rose and Bill ran stumbling and apologising in his path.

'Why's he running away?' Bill panted after Rose. 'Why doesn't he just squish us with this mask?'

Rose shook her head, still running, her breath coming in gasps. 'Perhaps he can't. No ceremony – yet. First time – he's worn it. He's not – strong enough.' She didn't add that Gossamer might be scared of Gus, she didn't quite like to say it out loud. There was a burning light in the cat's eyes, the orange and the blue shining like jewels. He looked ready to tear Gossamer to pieces.

'Don't let him out of your sight,' Gus hissed over his shoulder, but it was difficult – the night outside the palace was dark and moonless, lit only by huge burning torches that were set in brackets around the walls. In the flickering circles of orange light, odd faces jumped and peered, and Rose saw that the streets were

full of dancers. Their costumes were ragged imitations of the satins and velvets inside the palace, and their masks had no jewels, but they danced with wild excitement. There was a faint echo of the music from inside the palace, and here and there someone played a flute or a violin, but many of the whirling figures seemed to be dancing to the insistent lapping of the sea against the quayside, or a tune that only they could hear.

'This is no good. Can't see a blasted thing.' Bill scrambled onto the base of a statue, and snatched one of the tar-soaked torches, leaping down again with it flaring above his head.

Gossamer had forced his way through the crowds, leaving the dancers staring after him in bewilderment, as though they did not know quite what had happened. Gus bounded after him, and Rose caught Bill's hand and chased them both. The torchlight wavered in the night wind as they ran, and here and there a startling angel appeared, as the fire lit up the mosaics along the cathedral walls.

'He's doubled back – he was trying to lose us in the crowds, so he could get back to the palace.' Gus stared up at them, his eyes sparkling wickedly. 'If we can keep him away, he'll miss the ceremony. Look, there! He's seen us. Now he's making for the quayside again.'

Gus leaped into Rose's arms, the fur rising along his spine as he stared out over the water. 'Yes. In that gondola. It's hard to see, but that must be his ship they're rowing out to.' His eyes glittered. 'Good, good, we're driving him away from the palace.'

'How are we going to follow him?' Bill looked around. There were hundreds of gondolas and other craft tied up at the elegantly carved blue-and-gold mooring poles. But they had no money.

Gus sprang to the ground and stared at them, and Rose could have sworn he was smiling. Then his eyes grew even larger, the dark lines around them darker, and his whiskers glimmered. He gazed up at them tragically, and managed to look several pounds thinner.

'Yes, well,' Bill muttered reluctantly. 'Creature of the devil, you are, Mrs Jones always said so. Oh, don't look at me like that!'

Gus snorted with laughter, and trotted purposefully along the edge of the water, looking for a hopeful victim.

He pattered out along a wooden causeway, and mewed plaintively at a young gondolier, hardly older than Rose and Bill, who was sitting on the end of his gondola eating a hunk of bread and ham. Rose, waiting in the shadows a little way behind, felt sorry for him,

shivering in his black and gold jacket. A cold wind was biting as it cut across the water.

The boy laughed at the sight of Gus, and held out a piece of his bread and ham invitingly. Gus took it delicately between his teeth, and purred, then he climbed onto the boy's lap, and rubbed his whiskers lightly down the thin brown face. The boy trembled slightly, and rubbed his hand over his cheek in a bewildered fashion.

'He will do what he is told,' Gus said to Rose in a low voice.

'Except he won't understand a word we say!' Bill pointed out.

'Get into the boat. Rose will tell him.'

Rose and Bill scrambled into the gondola, and the boy, who looked dazed, untied the mooring rope, and began to pole them out away from the causeway.

'Hold the torch in front of his face,' Rose whispered to Bill, but he turned to her worriedly. 'What are you going to do?' he demanded.

'Nothing bad! What do you think I am? I just want to show him the ship!'

Bill sniffed, but he turned back and held up the torch, and beckoned to their gondolier. 'Hey!'

The boy frowned, but then his mouth dropped open, and he almost let go of the oar, muttering under

his breath, and casting an awed glance at Rose, before he went back to gazing at the torch.

It was smoking now, the tarry wood sending off a black odd-smelling cloud, which formed itself into a sailing ship, and sped off across the lagoon.

'Follow it!' Bill pointed, stabbing urgently in the direction of the smoke-ship. 'Go! Go!'

The boy spoke no English, but he understood that clearly enough, and set off, digging his oar fiercely into the water, leaving a creamy swirl of bubbles.

Gossamer's ship was anchored out where the water was deeper. It was silent, with no sailors on the deck, and only one lantern lit, shining in the window of the stern cabin.

'How are we going to get on board?' Rose murmured, as the side of the ship towered above them.

Bill shook his head, but Gus padded along the back of the gondola to charm the boy again, nudging him gently to row around the ship to the anchor chain.

'You can't!' Rose hissed, as Gus perched on the side of the gondola, tensing his muscles to make the leap to the huge iron links. 'You'll fall!'

'I will not!' Gus stared back at her arrogantly.

Rose sighed. 'Please be careful. And wait for us! Find us – I don't know? A rope ladder?' She shivered at the

thought. 'Don't go chasing Gossamer without us, Gus, promise me!'

'I promise.' And he was gone, a swift white ghost flickering away up the chain.

They waited in the gondola, with the boy sitting curled up on the back, blinking confusedly at the dark water. Gus's spell seemed to be wearing off – clearly he was wondering where he was. Rose felt cold to the bone in only her silvery dress. Huddled out here against the black ship, the glittering, dancing city looked so very far away.

A hiss startled them, and something bumped down from above.

'It's a swing!' Bill reached up to catch it. 'Or something like it. How's he lowered it?'

They couldn't see, the slope of the ship's side was in the way, but Gus's head appeared over the edge, looking disconcertingly tiny, and a cry of 'Hurry!' floated down to them. 'And send the boy away.'

The gondolier was looking up at Gus, and frowning, as though he couldn't remember something. 'Thank you,' Rose murmured, wishing she had something to pay him with, or even just that he could understand how grateful she was. Sadly she untied the ribbons of her glittering mask, and gave the jewels a last little pat. She couldn't bear the thought of losing it, but it was all she had. She held it out to the boy, and he stared it at covetously, but shook his head, pushing it back to Rose, and giving her a graceful little bow. Rose smiled at him. 'Go. Please,' she whispered, pointing back towards the city. Oh, she wished she could make him understand. She didn't want this stranger mixed up in what they were going to do. She fixed her eyes on his, pleading, and he nodded reluctantly.

Then she climbed gingerly onto the wobbly rope contraption, and Bill squeezed next to her, holding the torch carefully out to the side.

'Hold on,' Gus mewed from above, and the whole thing bumped away up the side of the ship, Rose's heart bumping with it.

'Goodbye!' she whispered to the gondolier, and he began to pole his craft away. They could see his white smudge of a face looking back at them as they inched slowly upwards.

As they rose to the ship's balustrade and scrambled over, Rose gave a horrified squeak.

'Quiet!' Gus hissed back. 'Do you want him to hear us? And I couldn't do it by myself.'

Hanging onto the rope with hundreds of tiny claws were a gang of confused-looking rats, their tiny eyes blinking in a suspicious daze.

'What did you do to them?' Bill asked disgustedly.

Gus shrugged, and showed his teeth, and Bill

shuddered. As soon as both the children were safely on board, Gus snarled something, and the rats disappeared across the deck in a wave of dirty brown.

'So now what are we going to do?' Bill asked sceptically, and Rose shook herself. She had been staring after the rats, her fingernails digging into her hands. She hated them. They reminded her of the orphanage, where the rats had roamed the attic dormitories, almost as hungry as the children.

'He's in the lit cabin, isn't he?'

'You just want to walk in there?' Bill sounded incredulous. '*That's* your plan?'

'He cannot have failed to notice that we are here.' Gus was sitting on a coil of rope, washing his ears. He looked calm, but Rose was sure he only washed when he was worried.

'So…so why isn't he coming?' Rose looked over her shoulder to the companionway.

Gus stretched elaborately. 'Perhaps he is waiting to see what we will do.'

Bill was staring into the torch flame as though mesmerised. 'I think we should fire the ship.'

'No!' Rose protested, but Gus looked thoughtful, and Bill went on, more enthusiastically. 'We could lower a boat ready, so we get off safe, and he'd be trapped.'

'That's a horrible thing to do.'

Gus nodded. 'It is.' Then he looked over at Bill. 'Go and lower the boat.'

'You can't!'

'Rose, he's tried to kill you about three times. He's your enemy, don't you want to get rid of him?' Gus looked at her with narrowed eyes. 'If you're ever going to become a real magician, you're going to have to harden your heart.'

Rose kneeled down by the ropes to look into his face. 'I know we have to…' She swallowed. 'We have to kill him. But not like that…'

Suddenly Bill was there, reaching down a hand to pull her up. 'I've already done it. Get up, quick. You need to help me lower the boat down. Don't look at me like that. You were going to spend the next ten minutes fighting with your conscience, while that monster works out how to kill *us*. Anyway, Rose, don't be silly. He isn't just going to sit there and let himself be crisped, is he? But at least now he'll have to come out and fight, and the only way out is through that hatch.'

'And we have to fight him back, on a ship that's on fire!' Rose hissed, looking round furiously at the coil of rope that Bill had set alight with his tinder-box. It was smouldering, and little tongues of flame were starting to lick across the deck. 'What about the crew?'

Bill shrugged. 'There's no one here, Rose.'

The flames had leaped up now to one of the furled sails, and they were spreading fast, fanned by the wind. 'The old devil's going to have to come on deck soon,' Bill muttered. 'There's no other ways out, are there?'

'Only the stern cabin window…' Rose looked up at him, her eyes wide with horror, and then away to the back of the ship. 'He did! He climbed up!'

White fingers were gripping the ship's rail, horribly like bones. Rose moved closer to Bill, wondering what on earth they were going to do. The thrill of the chase, and her fury with this man who had killed her master, had brought her this far, but now she was suddenly aware that this was the magician who had cast London into winter, and snatched a princess away from her palace.

Gossamer heaved himself over the rail, and smoothed down his coat with those long pale fingers. He touched the mask delicately, checking that it was still in place. The white hands stroked the white cheek, and Rose shuddered. Then he strolled calmly through the flames, which sizzled and spat, as though he was casting buckets of water over them, and stood towering over the children.

'Was he that tall before?' Bill nudged Rose.

Rose shook her head. 'I think the mask is making

him different… He was right to be scared of it.' She was flickering her fingertips as she spoke, changing the hiding spell that Mr Fountain had taught them – for what would be the point of disappearing now, when Gossamer could see exactly where they were standing? Now, instead of misting them away, the spell would wrap them in a cloud of – well, Rose wasn't quite sure what, but hopefully something that would deflect any spells Gossamer tried to use.

She finished it, gasping, just in time. The tall masked figurc was pacing closer. He seemed thinner too, as though something had stretched him upwards. The mask was glowing now, with a strange bluish light that turned what could still be seen of Gossamer's face a sickly sort of colour.

'He most definitely does not have that mask under control,' Gus muttered, backing away, his tail fluffing up to double-size.

Suddenly, the blue light exploded out of the mask, filling the air with shards of ice, dagger-sharp, like flying needles.

Rose's protection spell did work, but not quite in the way she expected. Clearly the spell was ingenious, and she had asked it to protect them from whatever Gossamer might hurl at them. So the furled mizzen sail

collapsed over the top of them, covering them in tough sailcloth.

'Rose!' Bill sounded squashed.

'Sorry! I didn't mean it to do that.'

The edges of the enormous sail were already blackening as they crawled out from underneath, and after that it was burning in seconds, spreading the fire over the whole of the stern deck, melting the tar between the decking, and sending sizzling little spurts of flame over the wood.

'We never lowered the boat,' Bill muttered, looking over the side at the dark, cold water. 'We could jump, I suppose.'

'I'd rather burn,' Gus muttered, his eyes still fixed on Gossamer. 'What is he doing?'

The thin magician was holding his hands cupped in front of him, and somehow in them was water, black water, like the sea that was suddenly starting to surge around the ship.

'Is it him, making the water do that? Oh!' Rose lost her footing as the deck seemed to slip sideways, and then lurched back again.

'Water magic.' Gus sprang into Rose's arms. 'I suppose it's not much different to ice. And they're known for it here, of course. He must have been studying.'

'Criminy!' Bill was staring over Rose's shoulder, and Rose hastily followed his horrified glance. Coiling up into the sky above them was a tower of water, looking almost solid as it caught the light of the flames. It bobbed and danced on the surface of the sea, weaving perilously close to the ship.

'What's he's thinking? If he sends that against us, he'll be broken up too!' Bill backed up towards Rose and flung his arm around her shoulders.

The waterspout was mesmerising, spinning around the ship, coming closer and closer.

'He's mad,' Rose murmured, dragging her eyes away to look again at Gossamer.

He seemed hardly to have noticed the waterspout behind him, and his eyes were still fixed on that strange little handful of water. Rose pulled out of Bill's grip suddenly, and ran at him, clutching Gus tightly in one arm, and flinging up her other hand to dash the dark water away.

Gossamer howled, his eyes wild behind the mask, and hit her. One long white hand, still dripping with the enchanted water, struck her across the face, sending her flying over the deck.

Sobbing, Rose crouched against the rail, her fingers searching the tiny hanging pocket of her dress for the china doll. A little of her fear seemed to lift away when

her fingers closed around it. Even if he killed her, a tiny drop of her blood would be left behind inside that porcelain body, and that was a comfort somehow. Rose had a feeling that even if the doll fell to the bottom of the sea, she would be found, and in a little Venetian child's arms before too long. Wasn't there a story about a magic ring, thrown into the sea, only to be swallowed by a fish and delivered up for breakfast?

Dazedly, Rose shook the stories out of her head, and stared around her, trying to work out what was happening.

'Are you safe, Rose?' Bill was darting warily across the burning deck towards her. 'Did he hurt you?' He flung an arm around her, and they staggered together as the ship rocked, shaking as if it had collided with another vessel.

The waterspout had collapsed into a foaming mass of spray, and Gossamer fell on his knees on the deck, moaning, and trying to catch the water droplets as they sizzled into the fire. Then he stood up – or rather, the mask pulled him up, so he looked like a gigantic leggy puppet. And then he came stalking across the fiery deck to Rose.

Still shaken from her fall, she stared up at him, dimly hearing Bill shouting vain threats. Gus was standing over them hissing defiantly, but he seemed so small against the black figure loping towards the children.

Rose moaned in horror. Rising from the ship's timbers behind Gossamer was another waterspout – or so it seemed at first. A black column of water and smoke, grown from Gossamer's enchanted handful, and the fire of the ship, woven together by the power of the mask.

'That's not his work,' Gus mewed, his claws scrabbling nervously on the deck. 'That's the mask, all by itself. There's no smell of him in it.'

'He should never have tried to use it,' Rose whispered. 'I don't think he's really there at all. Oh!'

'What is that?' Bill was behind her, his livery jacket charred by falling embers from the burning rigging, and a red streak across his face. He crouched next to her, one hand on Gus's coat. The fire was all around them, but something far more dangerous was growing above Gossamer now.

The black shape dwarfed the magician it was draining. A huge dragon made of water and smoke and fire, and it was growing to the height of the mainmast. The creature roared a burning breath, then reached out one flaming claw and seized Gossamer, so that he hung limply, his legs faintly waving, the puppet of the mask.

'I've changed my mind.' Gus turned to Rose and Bill. 'We jump. Now, while it's occupied with him.'

He raced to the rail, the fire glittering on his white fur, so that for a second he was a glowing marmalade cat. Bill pulled Rose up, and they stumbled after him.

Rose's head swam as she looked down at the water so far below, already sizzling as gouts of burning tar dripped from the ship's side. Then Gus climbed onto her shoulders, and seemed to grow impossibly heavy, and she was falling, falling towards the blackness.

It was so cold it burned, more than the fire, and Rose sank under the water, her hair coming unpinned and floating in a cloud about her face. Strange creatures seemed to swirl around her, mermaids mingling their hair with hers, and a grinning, toothy water sprite, who resolved himself into Gus, his paws threshing frantically against the water.

Rose felt a sudden and horrible aching inside her as her body fought for air, and she twisted in panic, her fingers clenching desperately around the doll. The chill of the china skin softened in the water, and now the hands were bigger, and they were holding Rose's, not the other way around. It was pulling, pulling, dragging Rose towards the flickering lights above. Gasping and spitting Rose fought herself upwards, the delicate little hands of the doll leading her on.

But when she splashed out of the water, shaking herself like a half-drowned dog, there was no china-white girl there with her, only Gus, coughing furiously. Rose gazed around her, bewildered. Had she imagined it? The tiny creature in her hand was only a porcelain doll again, and there was no sign that it had been anything else. Except perhaps that its painted smile seemed wider in the starlight.

Somehow it seemed colder than ever now they had broken the surface at last, and Gus's claws tangled in her hair. He looked half-drowned, and huddled against her coughing.

'Bill! Bill!' Rose had never swum in her life, but she seemed to be able to float, although she had no idea how they were to get to shore. The burning ship was some distance away now, but the lights of the city were even further.

'I'm here,' someone spluttered, and a bedraggled pile of rags, clutching a half-burned spar, kicked towards her. Bill's hair was lying flat for once, plastered to his forehead with water. 'The ship's breaking up. Look! There goes that thing!'

Spiralling into the night sky went the fire dragon, and the ship exploded as it left the deck.

'It still has Gossamer, I think,' Rose murmured, gripping tightly onto the spar with Bill.

Gus, now balancing on her shoulder out of the water, craned his neck around, and nodded. 'I can see

him in its claws. But – he looks dead. Ah! It's dropping him!'

There was the faintest splash, and the limp black bundle slid horribly quickly under the water, and was gone.

THIRTEEN

The boy poled them swiftly through the water, every so often casting wondering glances back towards the burning ship.

The gondola had come gliding towards them a few minutes after the dragon had disappeared. The boy had obviously seen it – the whole city must have done – and he had come back for them, muttering prayers of relief as he hauled them out of the water. He had forced them to drink out of a small black bottle that he had concealed in an inside pocket of his jacket, spirits that burned Rose's throat wonderfully as she swallowed and coughed.

They scrambled out at the quayside, and Gus, looking half his usual size, purred loudly at the boy. He

glanced up at Rose, and whispered, 'Pull out one of my whiskers, and give it to him.'

Rose winced, but did it anyway, passing the thin white wire to the staring gondolier. 'Keep it safe,' she told him, folding his fingers around it, and pressing his hand against her own heart. 'For luck, you see?' And he nodded, wide-eyed, and kissed his fingers to her and Gus.

Then they slipped through the muttering crowd, all watching the ship as it burned down closer and closer to the water line.

The masquerade was over, and no music came from the palace windows. Half the lights were out, and a yawning guard was more interested in gazing out at the fire than he was in them.

'We missed that ceremony, then, I reckon,' Bill murmured, as they slid past the guard.

Rose nodded. She wasn't sure whether to be glad or sorry. They had stopped Gossamer joining himself to the mask, at least. She had a feeling that if he'd tried to take part in the ceremony, the power of the mask might have swallowed up the whole palace, and them with it. But she wished she'd seen what happened, after all those strange stories.

They crept back through the palace, making for the staircase, and dreading what they would find. They had beaten Gossamer – there was no doubt in their minds that he was gone, and the mask had gone with him, dragging him down into the water. It was back where it belonged, at least, and the bottom of the lagoon seemed the safest place for it to be. But that triumph seemed useless now, when they were going back to find Mr Fountain's body.

Rose felt deathly tired as they stumbled along the passage to the staircase. Her soaked dress clung to her, and she was so cold. The brilliant lights of the palace seemed only to make it worse, and Gus was trembling.

When the duke walked up from the head of the staircase, Rose thought he might be a dream, some sort of odd vision that her cold mind had conjured up. But when Miss Fell followed him, and then a pair of servants carrying Mr Fountain in a litter made out of a torn-down tapestry, she blinked and realised that this was real. Gus leaped out of her arms, and went running towards his master, as Miss Fell directed the servants with her cane.

'Here, lay him down here, where the light is better. I cannot work in that gloom you keep in those lower passages, Your Grace.'

The duke bowed, almost apologetically, and Rose glanced at Miss Fell, wondering if he'd been set free from his enchantment.

The old lady continued. 'Really, I don't know what you think you were doing, letting those dangerous criminals lurk about the city. And even in the palace! I know the history of the place is picturesque, but surely we are beyond such things in these modern times. It was very lax of you.'

Rose kneeled beside the litter as Miss Fell continued to harangue the duke. Bella and Freddie held Mr Fountain's hands, and he was deathly white, but she could see that he was still breathing.

'We caught him, sir,' she whispered. 'The mask destroyed him, he's at the bottom of the lagoon – the mask too.'

She was almost sure his eyelids fluttered, but he said nothing.

The cracked old voice went on. 'You will have to deal with your brother, you know. You were quite bewitched! It was an attempt to seize the throne, you cannot deny it this time.'

The duke sighed, and shrugged very slightly. Rose had a horrible feeling that Girolamo might already have been dealt with.

'Your hair now, Isabella dear.'

Rose blinked, wondering if she was imagining things again, but Miss Fell held out a tiny pair of golden scissors to Freddie, and he cut off a long lock of Bella's golden hair. Bella the vain hardly seemed to notice.

When Miss Fell pulled out a pair of white bone knitting needles, Rose simply leaned back against the wall and watched. She was no longer sure if she was asleep or awake. The old magician began to knit Bella's hair, chanting the pattern of the stitches under her breath.

'*Knit one, purl one, knit two together, slip, slip and breathe. Cast on another year, and increase.*' The needles clicked together busily, and Rose's vision blurred. She watched Miss Fell lay her glistening knitting over the hilt of the knife, and then someone shook her.

'Rose, you have to help hold the knife. We have to pull it out together, you, me and Bella. Rose, wake up!' Freddie sounded as exhausted as she was, which was hardly fair – he hadn't encountered any dragons, and he wasn't all wet.

'Wake up!'

'I am awake!' she protested. She was only cold, that was all.

'Come, dear child.' Someone lifted her up, and a rich, caramelly voice murmured in her ear.

'You speak English!' Rose stared up at the duke indignantly. 'But you made us think you didn't understand a word we said!'

The duke smiled. 'You have work to do.'

Bella pulled Rose over to her father, and placed her icy hand on the hilt of the knife with her own and Freddie's. 'Why are we pulling it out?' Rose whispered wearily. 'Won't he bleed to death? We said we mustn't...'

'But we have the spell now, Rose,' Bella snapped impatiently. 'Miss Fell is going to knit him back together. Come on!'

The knife made Rose even colder – the metal seemed to have sealed itself to her fingers, as though they would blister and tear when she tried to pull them away.

'Now pull,' Bella whispered, and Rose cried out as the bespelled metal bit into her skin, sending a thousand snowflakes whirling through her veins. But the blade was easing slowly out of their master's chest, leaving a horrid unnatural hole. Dark blood began to well out of it immediately, but then that strange lacy knitting, hair-fine, slid down the blade and smothered the cut, the blood dying Bella's fair hair pink. Bella's tears fell and glittered on it like crystals, so that the whole thing resembled an expensive scarf that some rich Venetian lady would drape around her elbows for a ball.

'Is it working?' Freddie looked up hopefully at Miss Fell.

'What do we do with this?' Rose was holding the knife now, its blade no longer burning her, but glinting dully in her hand, like some ancient weapon chipped out of stone. A faint cast of red washed over it, as she turned it in her hand. Blood again, like the masked boys' knives. But this time she hadn't done it, had she? She shivered, and figures swam to the surface through the redness. Figures in uniform. Men on horseback. Rushing towards each other, screaming. And then lying still, in a quiet field.

'What was that?' she whispered, but no one else had seen.

'I will take it.' The duke lifted it out of her hand. 'It would be best destroyed.'

Rose nodded, although she wasn't sure if that meant he was actually going to destroy it or not. The duke handed the knife to one of his lackeys, who disappeared with it rather quickly, in case anyone might be about to argue. The duke smiled like velvet at Rose when he saw her watching, and gave her a slight, respectful nod.

'A very valuable artefact, dear Miss Rose,' he murmured.

'Did you catch him?' Mr Fountain's voice was faint and whispery, but everyone in the passageway turned, transfixed.

'Yes. Yes, we did. Well – he got dropped in the sea by a dragon, and we're practically certain he's dead,' Rose added, wanting to be accurate.

'He looked dead,' Gus agreed, nudging Mr Fountain's chin lovingly.

'He must be.' The duke nodded. 'Our esteemed Miss Fell almost had me free, but traces of the enchantment were lingering. Until suddenly they disappeared, like *that*!' He snapped his fingers, and gave them a wolfish smile. 'When he died.'

Mr Fountain sighed. Then he added thoughtfully, 'And I'm *not* dead?'

'Don't be stupid, Aloysius,' Miss Fell snapped.

'I was just checking,' he told her humbly, and then he lay back, smiling to himself, and the hole in his waistcoat sewed itself together again, with even fancier embroidery than before.

FOURTEEN

The ship was far grander than the one they had sailed across the channel on, and even the sailors wore an elegant striped livery, and snow-white trousers.

It seemed to cut through the water at an incredible speed, running before the wind under full sail.

'I had hardly believed these things existed,' Mr Fountain mused, staring up at the full load of sail on the three masts. 'A fairy tale, that's all. No wonder the Arsenal has such high walls, with secrets such as this behind it. Twice as fast as it should be, at least. What the Lords of the Admiralty wouldn't give…' He sighed. 'I should think it'll be gone in minutes, once we dock at Dover. They won't be letting those nosy Royal Navy types get anywhere near.'

Talis was mobilising its troops, Venetian spies had told the duke. Grand military 'displays' were being held in every town, on the vaguest of excuses, and the reserves were being called up. It had not been thought sensible for the little English party to travel home over land, and the duke wished to make it clear that he was grateful. His Grace had been left deeply in their debt, after they rescued him from Gossamer's spell. He had presented Mr Fountain with a heavily sealed document for the king, which Mr Fountain was keeping tucked inside his waistcoat. Every so often he slid a hand in to pat it lovingly, and a gloating little smile flitted over his face.

'What actually makes it go faster?' Rose asked, hanging over the side and staring at the wake creaming away behind them.

'If I knew that I'd be the richest man in England.' Mr Fountain coughed, and smiled to himself. 'Well. I'd be significantly richer, anyway. For a start, Rose, every plank has been put together with magic. Every rope, every scrap of sail. Enormous task. The number of magicians they must have had working on it. And fully half the crew must be magic-workers of some kind.'

'You would think that if they're that clever they could make it a smoother journey.' Miss Fell sniffed in a ladylike manner. 'Don't slop that beef tea, William.'

She refused to call him Bill.

'Oh no...' Mr Fountain stared at Bill, who was concentrating so hard on carrying the two-handled cup that his tongue was sticking out. But Bill glared back at him fiercely, and Mr Fountain sighed, and apparently decided it would be cruel to make him spill it.

'You *will* drink this.' Miss Fell eyed Mr Fountain beadily, and very much in the manner of an aunt. 'I have spent considerable time explaining the recipe to the cook, and I had to prevent him from adding all sorts of unsuitable things.'

'Flavour, possibly...' Mr Fountain muttered, as he sipped the beef tea with his eyes screwed up.

Miss Fell diplomatically ignored him, and seated herself graciously in the basket chair next to his. They had been given a small area of the stern deck as a sort of outdoor drawing room, as Miss Fell insisted that fresh air was vital to Mr Fountain's recovery. Accordingly, he was muffled from head to toe in blankets and made to sit outside even when it was snowing.

'Rose!' Miss Fell thumped her stick on the deck in a peremptory fashion, and Rose turned away from the rail at a run, before remembering and slowing to a decorous, ladylike trot.

Miss Fell watched approvingly. 'Good girl. Now.

It seems to me that a long sea voyage is the perfect opportunity to make sure that your education is progressing properly. It would be so easy for Aloysius to forget those elements of magic that are so important to a young lady. Pass me that work bag, my dear.'

Rose cast an anguished look at Mr Fountain, but he appeared to be asleep, in the most cowardly way, and Bella and Freddie were watching for whales on the other side of the deck. With the quietest of sighs, she passed the bag to Miss Fell.

'Now, have you been taught embroidery?'

Rose shook her head. 'Plain sewing only, ma'am. I can manage cross-stitch, but nothing fancy.'

Miss Fell tutted. 'I might have known. So short-sighted.' She glared at Mr Fountain, who emitted a well-timed snore. 'A young lady should always be able to embroider. And as a magician you will find it remarkably useful.' She gave Rose a sharp look as she handed her a piece of linen, and some rose-pink embroidery thread. 'Try a flower, perhaps. And don't even think of telling me that you are not a young lady.'

Rose shut her mouth with a snap.

'You are. Who knows what happened – an accident, some dreadful mishap...' She stared off into the distance, where grey sky met grey sea. 'We shall find out.'

'Will we?' Rose ran the needle sharply into her finger, and gasped.

'Tch. Don't stain the linen, girl. Some common sense, please. Of course we will.' She regarded Rose thoughtfully. 'Don't you want to?'

Rose sat staring at the drop of blood, rising like a jewel on her fingertip, and wondered. Whose blood was it, apart from hers? Did it matter? Did she even care? She had always promised herself she didn't, but that had been a way to survive the orphanage, without pretending to herself that she was really a lost duchess, as half the other girls did. Then it had been a defence against Susan and her cruel teasing about charity girls and changelings. Rose had *not* cared, fiercely.

But now she did. Why not admit it? She wanted a family who could make ships full of magic, or see messages in the stars.

Miss Fell watched her expectantly, the glittery old eyes following every expression that crossed Rose's face. She sat with her hands folded on her work bag, but one of the ivory knitting needles was twisted in her fingers, and it was starting to splinter.

Rose didn't see any of this. She was staring at Bella, leaning over the side, and laughing with Freddie. Was that what she wanted? To be a little lady? She thought of Bella, holding the hilt of the knife in her father's chest, her face anguished.

'I should like to know.' She nodded decisively. 'But whoever I really am, I shan't be anyone else apart from me. They gave me up, however it happened. So I don't belong to anyone, only myself, and I shall stay that way.'

Win a Tea Party with Holly Webb!

We are offering one lucky ***Rose*** fan the chance to have afternoon tea with Holly Webb. The prize will include afternoon tea for the winner, two friends and a parent or chaperone, and travel to the venue. Ten runners-up will receive a set of signed ***Rose*** books.

To enter the competition, all you have to do is visit

www.orchardbooks.co.uk/rose

and sign up.

Only one entry per person

Closing Date: **31st October 2010**

The winners will be chosen at random

Competition only available to UK residents.

For full terms and conditions go to www.orchardbooks.co.uk/rose